KILLER SPECIES
feeding frenzy

KILLER SPECIES
feeding frenzy

Michael P. Spradlin

SCHOLASTIC INC.

ISBN 978-0-545-50673-1

12 11 10 9 8 7 6 5 4 3 2 1   13 14 15 16 17 18/0

Printed in the U.S.A.   40
First printing, November 2013

The display type was set in Badhouse Light.
The text type was set in Apollo MT.
Book design by Nina Goffi

For my daughter,
Rachel Leigh Spradlin.
You never fail to make me smile.

KILLER SPECIES

feeding frenzy

August

FIVE HUNDRED YARDS OFFSHORE DR. CATALYST STOOD at the stern of a commercial fishing vessel as it bobbed gently at anchor. He watched a group of seven people on the beach through his binoculars. Early this morning he had left his current base and followed the tracking signals in the group's vehicles to this semi-deserted stretch of ocean beach. They had no idea he was observing them. In fact, it was likely they presumed him dead. If only they knew the vengeance he was about to unleash on them.

Dr. Catalyst rubbed his mangled right hand against his thigh. It had taken months to recover from the crushing bite of his Pterogator, received when those two little brats Emmet Doyle and Calvin Geaux stepped in to foil his plans. The severity of his injury had forced him to go to ground on the Seminole reservation deep in the River of Grass. There he had tried to heal under the care of his uncle, a tribal elder and doctor. But they had a vicious falling out. His uncle did not support Dr. Catalyst's methods for saving the environment. Finally, they argued so violently that his uncle banished him from the reservation forever. *Fool*. Dr. Catalyst was a genius. He was doing great things. Let them cast him out. When the time was right, he would destroy them, too.

His hand tapped harder and harder against his thigh until the discomfort forced him to stop. The constant pain he felt in his mangled limb was just one thing that little punk Emmet Doyle was going to pay for. Very soon.

As he made the final preparations to exact his revenge, he chuckled softly to himself. Dr. Catalyst was beyond wealthy. In the years leading up to the initiation of his plan to combat invasive species, he had acquired several bases of operation all over South Florida. The Geauxs and the Doyles thought they had defeated him. They would soon learn how wrong they were.

All morning he studied them from offshore as they cavorted in the sun, unaware of the gruesome fate that awaited them. Watching them only made Dr. Catalyst angrier. They had cost him dearly in money, time, and resources. Now they played on the beach as if nothing had happened, as if they hadn't tried to destroy him and his work.

But their great mistake had been in thinking the Pterogators were his only creation. Boa constrictors and pythons were not the only invasive species destroying the fragile South Florida ecosystem. And his alligator hybrids were not his only experiment. Dr. Catalyst believed in multitasking.

Here in the waters of Florida, the nonnative lionfish was devastating the coastal reefs. No one knew exactly how the fish had been introduced here. Its normal habitat was in the Pacific and Indian Oceans. Most likely, lazy and irresponsible aquarium owners had released it, ignorant of the destruction it could wreak in the nearby waters. Much in the same manner the giant snakes had been set free into the swamp.

As with the Pterogator, Dr. Catalyst had looked at the problem and devised a solution. The lionfish was a reef dweller and an aggressive fish. It drove off any competitors that might occupy the same habitat, gorging on the fish and mollusks that made their homes in the reefs. And when a reef was finally picked clean, the lionfish would move on to another, stripping it as well.

To counter the fish's aggressiveness, he had devised the perfect predators. And he had them here on his boat, about to be released. The world would soon know that Dr. Catalyst had returned.

He had modified the catch tank on the boat. Now he opened the hatch in the rear deck and looked down on his creations. The sun was almost directly overhead, and the light flashed off the creatures' flanks as they writhed and thrashed in the shallow water of the tank below him. One of them reared its head, opening its elongated mouth. Its jaws revealed row upon row of sharp teeth, long and pointed as nails. They stuck out of the creature's mouth at odd angles, giving it a terrifying appearance. Its jaws snapped shut and Dr. Catalyst winced, remembering the devastation such a bite could cause.

The tank held his new fish species in just enough water for them to remain alive until they were released. He pressed a switch and it opened a panel cut through the bottom of the tank and through the boat's hull, releasing his newest killer species into the ocean.

From his computer pad, he watched the signals from the small tracking devices he had attached to the dorsal fin of each of his beasts. They swam so fast and hard, he did not think the devices would remain attached for long, but on their initial release he wished to track their progress for as long as he could. Taking a moment to adjust to their new environment, the giant fish swam lazily in the water beneath his boat. Then, as their instincts commanded, they zoomed toward the reef, cutting through the water with powerful strokes.

The sea was crystal clear and shallow here, and he watched their long, sinuous bodies surging across the ocean floor. Small schools of fish scattered in fear, desperate to flee these loathsome beasts. Waters that were full of dozens of marine species just moments before now looked deserted.

He studied the shoreline again and saw that the five young people were putting on fins and masks. They were on their way into the water for snorkeling. Dr. Catalyst smiled.

They were about to have a very bad day.

2

"ALSO, THE POSSUM, SWAMP FOX, MARSH RABBIT, otters, and the Florida panther, which is my personal favorite," Emmet said. Ever since he and Calvin had encountered Pterogators in the Everglades, Emmet was obsessed with learning the name of every creature in Florida with teeth.

"Dude, I don't think a rabbit is going to eat you," Stuke said. "And besides —"

"Excuse me. I was listing the many things in Florida that *could* eat me. Especially if Dr. Catalyst gets his hands on them. What if he crosses a polar bear with a marsh rabbit? Huh? What then?"

Emmet Doyle stood on the sandy beach near Little Card Sound, surrounded by his friends Stuke, Riley, and Raeburn. All summer he'd thought about Montana, and how he wasn't going back there any time soon. School started in two weeks. The conversation with his father concerning a return to Montana had been brief.

"Dad, you said you were *temporarily* assigned to Florida. I don't understand why we can't go back to Montana, and you can return to saving the blue-breasted something or other," Emmet had said. Repeatedly.

"The agency isn't sending me back until we solve this problem. It's out of my hands," Dr. Doyle told him. By his tone of voice, you would have thought he was searching the supply closet for missing paper clips, not facing down ferocious flying alligators every day.

So no Montana. And now here he was, standing on sand made molten by the sun, sweating like a . . . something that sweated a lot.

"In addition to the excess number of toothy creatures in your state, I would also like to point out that I have never sweated so much in my life," he said to Stuke and the girls. "My sweat has perspiration." All of them chuckled and shook their heads at another of Emmet's rants.

The summer had dragged along. Since Calvin was up at the Seminole reservation for much of it, visiting his father's family, Emmet had spent a fair amount of time with Stuke, Raeburn, and Riley. Emmet liked hanging out with the gang, but he had also missed Calvin. And ever since Calvin had returned a couple of weeks ago, the boy had been . . . a little moody.

Emmet's dad and Dr. Geaux were still hard at work trying to undo the freak show Dr. Catalyst had unleashed in the Everglades. More and more of his hybrid Pterogators were popping up.

"At least those Pterogators are eating snakes," Riley said. "I heard someone on TV say the snake population is decreasing."

"According to my dad, it's going to get worse as the Pterogators keep breeding," said Emmet. "Dr. Catalyst said they were just clones, but Dad said that's one reason why cloning is so controversial, because these clones mutated and can breed. He also said a lot of stuff about corrupted enzymes and chromosomes. I think. Honestly, when he goes all scientist I breeze out. Anyway, they can change and adapt, and the next thing you know you have hungry monsters trying to eat anything in sight. They've been eating other alligators, birds, foxes, at least part of one airboat, and they tried to turn two of Dr. Geaux's rangers into a Bloomin' Onion appetizer. And that's why I've spent the entire summer ready to leave for Montana at a moment's notice."

Except he wouldn't be leaving today. Today he was actually having fun. Dr. Geaux and his dad had brought him, Calvin, and the gang to the beach. They had taken over a spot that was fairly deserted along its western edge and were spending the day playing volleyball, cooking out, and just enjoying themselves.

Apollo had come along, too, and this was his first trip to the ocean. The little mutt had been confused by it. He crept carefully across the sand, puzzled at the size of the giant dog dish before him. As the waves rolled in and covered his paws, he had darted backward, barking and growling, and then charged forward as they receded. After a few minutes of showing the water who was boss, he had tired of the exercise and was now curled up beneath the picnic table, fast asleep.

And then there was Calvin. Since he'd returned from the reservation he was even quieter than usual. Calvin was never someone you'd call a talker, but he apparently had additional levels of non-talkiness. While his friends were kicking a hacky sack around, Calvin was down by the shore, staring out at the water.

Dr. Geaux and Dr. Doyle were at the grill next to a picnic table, laughing and talking about something Emmet would probably find completely uninteresting. That was another thing. Ever since they'd arrived in Florida, Dr. Geaux and Dr. Doyle seemed to "hit it off," as his dad had called it. They had even gone out to dinner a few times. Emmet wasn't sure how he felt about it. It was just . . . weird. But he wasn't going to think about that right now.

"Hey, Dr. Geaux," Emmet said as she approached.

"Emmet! You getting hungry? Your dad is doing his best not to burn the hot dogs. And failing. But I'll intervene, don't worry," she said.

Dr. Geaux was nice. Emmet liked her. But she'd started getting overly cheerful whenever he was around. Like she was trying really hard to make *sure* he liked her. Emmet was positive this had something to do with her and his dad going to dinner.

"I'm sure Dad can manage a hot dog," he said. "I was just wondering if I could talk to you a minute?"

"Sure," she said. They left Dr. Doyle at the grill and strolled farther down the beach, where they could talk without being overheard by anyone.

"Is Calvin okay?" he asked her.

For just a fleeting second, Emmet spied a wave of sadness and worry flicker across her face. She replaced it quickly with a smile. But it was there. Her eyes traveled across the sand to where Calvin stood alone, the incoming water splashing over his feet.

"I think so. Why do you ask?"

"I don't know. He's just seemed . . . a little more quiet than usual since he came back from the rez." Raeburn was also a Seminole and always referred to the reservation as "the rez."

"Hmm. Yes. I suppose that's right. Whenever he visits, no matter how much he enjoys time with his aunts and uncles and cousins, it reminds him of how much he misses his dad. Plus, next spring he's going to be old enough to take part in the Green Corn Dance. It's an important ritual for a Seminole boy. Calvin is only half Seminole, but he's still part of the tribe. And his dad won't be there to participate. A male relative will have to stand in. It's just going to be hard for him."

"I didn't know that. You probably know Calvin's not a talker. But I guess that explains it. I was just worried something else was wrong. Wanted to help somehow if I could."

Dr. Geaux smiled. It was a nice, genuine smile. The normal kind, not the kind she used when she was trying to get him to like her. It sort of reminded him of how his mom used to smile.

"Emmet, that's a really nice thing for you to say. I want you to know that Calvin thinks a lot of you. He talks about you all the time. When he does talk, that is."

That surprised Emmet. "Really?"

"Yep. And he could really use a friend right now. And for heaven's sake, does he know Riley has a hopeless crush on him?"

"Yeah, he does," Emmet said. "Well, we've talked about it. Sort of. But he's . . . Calvin."

"Maybe you should all go snorkeling. That might help Calvin get out of his head a little."

"I was afraid you might say that," Emmet said. "And I'd be happy to help, I really would. But I've made a vow to never go into any body of water again. Not even a bathtub. I'm strictly taking showers now. Nothing eats you in a shower."

Dr. Geaux laughed. "I don't know about that. Have you ever seen the Alfred Hitchcock movie *Psycho*? It's a classic horror movie. You'll never think about showers the same way again. But honestly, Emmet, I think you're okay here. Give it a try. Sometimes you just have to get back on the horse."

Emmet shook his head. "If Dr. Catalyst is still out there, he'll probably figure out a way to combine a horse with a saber-toothed tiger. No offense to your home state, Dr. Geaux, but Florida is full of critters that want to eat me. So ixnay on the orkelsnay."

"Emmet, you kill me," Dr. Geaux said, laughing. "I don't think I've ever met a twelve-year-old with your sense of humor. But Dr. Catalyst is long gone. His boat was covered in blood. The Dade County medical examiner said it was unlikely anyone could survive that much blood loss. Give snorkeling a try. You'll be fine. In fact, you might find yourself enjoying it. Just a few yards out from shore here, there's a large reef. You'll see all kinds of beautiful fish."

Emmet took a deep breath. "Okay. But if there is something down there looking for an Emmet sandwich, I'm holding you responsible."

"You and your father crack me up. Alligators don't come into salt water. You're good."

"My dad cracks you up?"

"Yes! He's hilarious."

"My dad? Dr. Benton Doyle? Bird Nerd Doyle is funny?"

"Haven't you heard yet that nerds are cool? And actually, yes, he's quite a comedian."

Emmet couldn't figure this out. What could his dad have possibly said to Dr. Geaux that was funny? Or even mildly humorous? *Knock-knock. Who's there? Peregrine. Peregrine who? That's a nice pair of green socks you're wearing.* Huh.

"All right. I'm going to get Calvin to take us snorkeling. He likes a project if he's in charge. But I'm entering the ocean under protest. If something down there —"

"There's nothing down there," Dr. Geaux interrupted him. "Don't worry. You'll be just fine."

3

EVERYONE DONNED FLIPPERS AND MASKS. THEY ALSO wore flotation vests because Dr. Geaux and Calvin were sticklers about safety. The vests provided enough buoyancy to keep a swimmer on the surface of the water, but weren't so bulky it made it hard to dive.

"Wouldn't it be cool if we found the *Black Thunder* out there?" Stuke asked.

"Don't be ridiculous, Stuke," Riley said. "That's just a story."

"What's Black Thunder?" Emmet asked. "Some kind of rogue shark?"

Raeburn laughed. "No. It's a legend about a haunted pirate ship. Supposedly it sunk somewhere nearby, with a fortune in gold aboard. A notorious pirate named

One Leg Sterling captained it. He had just raided a British man-of-war and taken on a lot of gold coins. His ship was damaged in the battle, though, and a sudden storm came up. The extra weight of all that gold caused it to sink, supposedly near here. Treasure hunters have been searching for the wreck for years. People say they sometimes see a pirate walking along the shore during the full moon — that it's Sterling looking for his lost treasure. But it's just a myth." Everyone had put on their snorkeling gear, and Emmet stared at the water. Far offshore a fishing boat bobbed at anchor.

Emmet felt something on his shoulder and jumped. Luckily it was only Calvin, not a ghost pirate or a Pterogator.

"Are you all right, dude? You look a little pale," Calvin said. He knew how skittish Emmet was about the water now.

"Don't do that!" Emmet complained.

"Do what?" Calvin asked, seriously confused.

"Don't sneak up on me like that. I could have gone all ninja on you," Emmet said. In addition to visiting the library nearly every day for a thorough study of Florida's fauna this summer, Emmet had insisted his dad enroll him in a karate class. Even though no one agreed with him, he still believed Dr. Catalyst was out there creating a giant opossum that knew kung fu. Emmet wanted to be ready.

"I wasn't sneaking up on you, I was standing right here. And I didn't know you'd made it all the way to ninja in two months of classes," Calvin said. Emmet was reasonably sure he was joking, but you could never tell with Calvin.

"You sneaked. You definitely sneaked. And okay, I'm a little leery about going in the water," Emmet said. "But I've got mad ninja skills now, so don't test me."

"What do you say we snorkel?" Calvin stalked off toward the water, walking awkwardly in his flippers.

"Okay. Snorkeling. It'll be fun. Let's follow Calvin. Nothing to worry about. Water's not that deep and stuff. No problem," Emmet said as he cautiously traipsed toward the water. The others seemed to walk easily into the ocean in their flippers, but Emmet lifted each foot and carefully stepped along like he was wearing giant clown shoes. At least it was warm. Warm water was probably better for sharks, though, and stingrays, giant squid, and killer whales.

"Hurry up," Calvin hollered. "We need to stay together."

Emmet quickened his pace and soon joined the others in waist-deep water. Everyone dived forward and swam out together.

Calvin was carrying a dive flag and swam a short distance ahead of them. A small weight was attached to the flag by rope, and he lowered it until it settled on the bottom. The bright red flag had a white stripe running at an angle across it. It was attached atop a small plastic float, which bobbed gently on the water. The flag would let any passing boaters know there were divers in the area. In Florida, it was illegal to snorkel or scuba dive without a dive flag. Calvin was a law-and-order guy.

Emmet was new to snorkeling but got the hang of it pretty quickly. It wasn't really swimming. It was mostly floating until something interesting appeared, then diving for a closer look, and staying down for as long as possible while holding his breath. Upon surfacing he blew the water out of his snorkel. Emmet found he could float for a long time, breathing through the plastic tube and observing the sea life.

The five of them floated in a rough semicircle, looking down into the waters below them. Emmet had to admit it was pretty spectacular. The water was a deep sky-blue color, and there were lots of cool fish and plants to look at. Parts of the coral reef were covered with indentations on the surface that made him think of pictures of the moon he'd seen in science class. Other parts stretched out like vibrantly hued fingers reaching into the ocean, or silk fans that swayed lazily in the currents. Emmet couldn't believe there were this many different colors under the water. Oranges, yellows, reds — and not just on the reef and the plants, but on the fish as well. It was a revelation to him, because he had never been in the ocean before. He understood now what Dr. Geaux had been trying to tell him. It was like nothing he'd ever seen.

He recognized a few of the fish swimming around, including a small school of groupers floating a few yards away near the surface. But around the reef itself there were hundreds of scary fish. They were reddish-orange with white stripes, and had sharp, dangerous-looking spines sticking out all over.

Emmet raised his head and tapped Raeburn on the shoulder. She looked up at him as they treaded water.

"What are those spiny fish? They look like they belong on the head of a medieval weapon," he said.

"They're lionfish," she said, shaking her head.

Great! Emmet thought. *In Florida even the fish are named after things that eat you.*

"Why did you shake your head?" he asked, glancing around to see Stuke had floated away from the group and Riley was trying to get Calvin's attention by pointing at something beneath the water.

"They're nonnative. An invasive species, just like the pythons Dr. Catalyst was trying to get rid of," she said. "They're really aggressive and they sting, so don't get too close."

"Of course they sting. It's probably fatal," Emmet said.

Raeburn shook her head. "No, it just hurts. They

chase off the other fish that feed around the reefs and then strip the reefs clean. They never recover."

"Can't they be caught or something? Like in nets?"

"They're too deep for nets, and they're hard to catch. Divers will sometimes spear them, and they can be eaten if you clean them right, but there are just too many of them now."

"Huh," Emmet said. "How are you so smart about all this stuff again?"

"It's called studying, Emmet. You should try it some-time," Raeburn said. She adjusted her mask and dived under the surface.

Emmet decided to follow her.

4

DR. CATALYST DONNED HIS WET SUIT AND SCUBA GEAR. He pushed a switch on the console near the ship's wheel for the proximity alarm. If a swimmer or another boat approached while he was in the water, a special watertight communicator on his wrist would vibrate a warning. He wasn't going to allow anyone to stop him this time, not the U.S. Coast Guard or those brats Emmet and Calvin.

Double-checking to make sure his tanks were full of air, he buckled himself into the rig and rolled backward off the boat. Also attached to his wrist was an underwater video camera. This time he would have to film his creations' first successful deployment from beneath the water.

Unlike with his Pterogators, Dr. Catalyst would not be able to return the Muraecudas to his base. They were not as trainable. They would stay free in the ocean, ridding it of the venomous pests. He was certain they would clear the reefs of lionfish in a matter of months.

Some scientists in Honduras had attempted to train sharks to feed on lionfish, but with only limited results. Since lionfish were reef dwellers, he had thought long and hard about what could thin their numbers.

Barracudas fed on the fish that congregate on or near reefs. Moray eels made their nests among the nooks and crannies of the coral. And the reef shark was able to sit still upon the ocean floor waiting for prey to swim into its territory. It was the ideal combination.

And now he had the perfect set of test conditions. A reef full of lionfish, according to reports from the Florida fisheries' records. And a group of obnoxious kids. He was certain the Muraecudas would ravage the lionfish. But what would happen if the nearby humans approached them?

Dr. Catalyst hadn't a clue. But he was anxious to find out.

5

THE SCHOOL OF GROUPERS DARTING AWAY FROM THE reef was the first indication something was wrong. And of course it was Calvin, the King of the Wild Frontier, who noticed it initially. He surfaced, hollering and waving his arms. Emmet, Riley, and Raeburn were floating nearby and raised their heads, treading water and looking at him quizzically.

"Where's Stuke?!" Calvin asked, swimming over to them. Looking around, they saw their friend about thirty yards farther out, almost directly over the top of the reef.

"Stuke!" Calvin shouted. But Stuke didn't hear them.

"What's wrong?" Emmet asked.

"The groupers. They swam off. Fast," Calvin answered.

"Calvin. We've talked about this. I need more infor —" Emmet said.

Riley interrupted. "When a school of fish swims off like that, it usually means there's a predator approaching."

"Probably just a marlin or a barracuda. Sharks don't usually feed this time of day," Calvin said. Emmet knew he was saying that for his benefit. But Calvin looked nervous. "We'll get Stuke and swim back to shore."

"Good idea," Riley said. She lifted her wrist and showed a plastic underwater camera attached to it. "I already got some great pictures, anyway."

They tried calling out to Stuke, but his head was beneath the water and he didn't hear them.

"All right, let's stay together and go get him," Calvin said, pulling his mask back into place. The four of them swam along the surface toward Stuke, but Calvin stopped suddenly. They all pulled up, treading water.

"What is it?" Emmet asked. He really didn't like the way this outing was progressing.

"I thought I saw . . ." Calvin put his face down in the water again.

"Oh, I hate when he does that," Emmet said. "What, Calvin? You thought you saw what?"

Calvin rose again, a look of alarm on his face.

"Stuke! Stuke!" he shouted. "Everybody, swim to him as fast as you can! Stay together."

Emmet was now officially frightened. The four of

them spat out their snorkels and swam as hard as they could toward Stuke.

Emmet couldn't resist, though. He ducked his head beneath the surface.

And immediately wished he hadn't.

Converging on the reef from farther out in the ocean were half a dozen creatures. They looked like something out of his worst nightmare. They swam toward the reef, their bodies long and slithering, almost like snakes, except their blunt faces held huge mouths full of needlelike teeth, sticking out all over. Row upon row of them flashed in the sunlit water.

They lunged through the water as they converged on the reef and tore into the lionfish. It was a feeding frenzy. Their heads and jaws snapped and slashed, devouring fish after fish, spines and all. The lionfish tried to scatter, but the creatures — each ten or twelve feet long — swam them down, devouring them.

Somehow Emmet's legs kept pumping. He knew on some level he was still swimming in Stuke's general direction, but he couldn't tear his eyes away from the carnage happening below him. The things were fast and flexible, and it was almost like they worked in concert, circling around any group of lionfish trying to escape and driving them back toward the reef.

In the minute or so it had taken them to swim this far, it appeared to Emmet the reef was wiped clean of lionfish, unless one had managed to cower under a rock somehow. The beasts were remarkable in their efficient savagery. He was about to raise his head up and ask Calvin what they were.

But right at that moment, one of them turned and spotted Stuke, who was snorkeling with his back to what had just transpired. With a mighty thrust of its snakelike body, it surged through the water.

Heading directly toward Stuke.

6

DR. CATALYST WAS MORE THAN A HUNDRED YARDS away from the group of swimmers. His camera was running, and he was delighted by what he'd just witnessed. The Muraecudas had cleared an entire reef of lionfish in minutes. It was astonishing, and they had done it with remarkable efficiency. Were he not underwater and breathing through his regulator, he would have been laughing with glee.

Now he kept the camera rolling, for one of the beasts had spotted a swimmer who was separated from the others by a fair distance. At this range it was impossible to tell which of them it was, but he hoped with all his heart it was that insufferable little snot Emmet Doyle. He flexed his damaged arm, remembering the combination of shock and outrage he'd felt when Emmet induced Hammer, one of his Pterogators, to attack him. More than the physical pain was the mental anguish. Years of work and research nearly destroyed. The fact that his hybrids were still active in the swamp provided the only solace.

Dr. Catalyst did not give up. For a reason he could not explain, he believed Emmet and he were connected somehow. Someone as brilliant as he would of course require a far more fearsome adversary, but he was no fool. Human history was full of instances when a younger, weaker, but plucky adversary had managed to defeat a superior foe.

But while Dr. Catalyst might be Goliath, Emmet Doyle was no David. Dr. Catalyst's work, his intelligence, was far too important and vast to be undone by a mere child, even one with as much sand as Emmet Doyle.

Dr. Catalyst peered through the lens of the video camera. The monster fish was almost upon the lone swimmer, and the other four tried desperately to alert him. Let them all be attacked and driven off. It would make good video. And it would show the world that this time, Dr. Catalyst meant business.

This footage would work perfectly for his next news release. He had engineered a new species: fast, aggressive, and it attacked swimmers! Tourists and locals alike would flee the ocean and all of South Florida! His creations could clear out the lionfish population, and with his Pterogators still on the loose in the Everglades, he would be one step closer to his goal.

Emmet Doyle, Dr. Geaux, all of them would see he could not be stopped.

It was perfect.

7

ONE MINUTE STUKE WAS FLOATING GENTLY IN THE water, and the next he was yanked beneath the surface by a hard tug on his leg. The pain hit him like a bolt of lightning. His head came up out of the water, and he screamed.

Stuke furiously kicked his foot, but something had hold of his leg and would not let loose. Worse, it was angrily shaking and writhing. Whatever it was, each time he moved, its teeth clamped down harder. The pain was excruciating. Still Stuke pumped his legs back and forth, desperately trying to free himself from whatever held him. He thought he heard voices calling to him, and shouts coming from the beach. But all his focus was on not passing out from the sudden, searing fire in his leg. If he didn't stay conscious, he would certainly drown.

The creature yanked hard again on his leg. Stuke screamed as it pulled him underwater. There was no time to hold his breath. His mouth filled with seawater, and he choked on the salty taste. Feeling weak and woozy, he tried kicking at whatever was dragging him — probably a shark — but it was too strong. As he sank in the water, he watched widening billows of red swirl around him and realized it was his blood. Now he was truly terrified.

When he looked down, his fear and confusion only worsened. His goggles were full of seawater and he couldn't see clearly. The creature holding him was big, but it wasn't a shark. It looked like a giant snake or maybe a huge eel. Whatever it was, its teeth were like shards of broken glass slicing into his flesh. He worried now that if the thing bit him any harder it would break his leg. He was more scared than he'd ever been in his entire life.

Stuke struggled, but he was losing his strength. His lungs burned and when the creature clamped down again, he opened his mouth to scream but only took in a mouthful of seawater. This was it. His parents' faces flashed in his mind, and he thought about how much he would miss them. He closed his eyes. With his last bit of oxygen and strength he gave his leg one more shake, but it was no use. He was going to drown, devoured by whatever strange beast held him in its grip.

The next thing he felt was hands under his arms, tugging him upward. He opened his eyes to see Calvin and Raeburn desperately trying to lift him to the surface. Calvin let go and swam right down to the creature, kicking out with his foot and landing blow after blow on its midsection. It didn't seem to even notice. And as each kick connected, it shook Stuke's leg and he writhed in pain. If anything, the monster clamped down harder. Stuke felt his body going limp. His friends could not save him.

Raeburn tore off her mask and snorkel, grabbing the hard plastic tube and holding it like an ice pick. She dived downward and stabbed it hard into the creature's eye. The creature was determined not to release its prey and tried to wiggle its body away from the persistent girl. Raeburn stabbed again and again and again, annoying the giant eel and causing Stuke to silently suffer in pain. As each blow landed, the creature tried to pull him deeper into the depths. With one last mighty swing, Raeburn furiously jabbed the creature in its now-bloody eye.

Finally, Stuke was free. The giant eel backed away and floated motionlessly a moment, as if stunned by its own pain. For a tense moment, it looked like it was going to strike at Stuke again. But it dived, slinking along the sandy bottom, trailing a stream of blood behind it. Two other dark shapes darted from the reef and followed the bloody path through the water.

Raeburn and Calvin grabbed Stuke beneath the arms and pumped their legs furiously toward the surface. When they broke through, Stuke spat out a stream of water, coughing and choking.

Calvin turned Stuke's head to the side. "Come on, Stuke! You gotta breathe, man!" he shouted. Stuke's head lulled forward and another stream of seawater cascaded out of his mouth. Finally, he took a huge, gasping breath. Then he screamed in agony.

"Ahh! My leg!" he shouted.

By then Emmet and Riley had arrived.

"Come on!" Emmet shouted. "We've got to get him to shore. Riley, you swim alongside him and help hold him up. Raeburn, put pressure on the wound and help Riley push him toward shore."

Emmet's legs worked furiously as he treaded water. He looked toward the beach to find his dad and Dr. Geaux staring at them with their hands shading their eyes, trying to determine what had happened. Apollo, who had been leashed to the picnic table so he wouldn't wander off, was in a full-on barking frenzy.

"Dad! We need help!" Emmet shouted. "Hurry! Stuke's hurt!"

"Go! Go! Go!" he shouted to his friends. The four of them kicked toward shore, moving clumsily, with Stuke thrashing and moaning in obvious pain. Dr. Geaux and his dad ran into the water fully clothed, splashing toward them.

"Calvin, you and I will guard the rear," Emmet said. He pulled his snorkel free from his mask like Raeburn had done, and Calvin did the same.

"We've got to watch so they don't attack us from behind," Emmet said.

Calvin understood immediately, and they both took deep breaths. Diving below the surface, they swam backward, their bodies at an angle to the ocean floor. At first it appeared as if the creatures had all disappeared. But then Emmet spotted two of them swimming hard along the sandy bottom, and veering in their direction. The trail of blood streaming from Stuke's leg was acting like a homing beacon for these creatures, and for who-knew-what else. Emmet remembered reading that sharks could smell blood in the water from great distances.

He and Calvin surfaced for air.

"Did you see them?" Calvin asked.

"Yeah. It's like they're circling. They're attracted by the scent of the blood," he said.

Stuke moaned in agony and Raeburn tried to comfort him. Riley was grunting with the effort of pulling him toward the shore. There were still about fifty yards between them and Dr. Geaux and Dr. Doyle, who were now swimming toward them.

"Okay," Calvin said. "Let's go under, find out where they are. I guess if they come at us, kick at 'em with our flippers. Maybe the splashing water will distract them. Better to lose a foot than a hand." He said it like losing a limb was a choice between regular and diet soda.

"I don't want to lose either!" Emmet said. But they both ducked beneath the surface. It was just in time. Two of the creatures were only yards away, and closing fast. All Emmet could see were wide-open mouths full of teeth the size of knitting needles. Both boys flipped onto their backs and kicked out with their legs, their swim fins thrashing through the water, causing it to swirl and surge around them.

It worked. At least this time. Unsure of what they were facing, the things broke off and dived toward the bottom again. The water was getting shallower as they drew nearer to the shore. Emmet realized he was getting tired. He took a breath and ducked back beneath the water, glancing all around, but found no sign of the eels.

"I think they're gone," he said, gasping as he and Calvin broke the surface.

"I don't know," Calvin said. "We better . . ." He

stopped. Their feet had touched bottom and their parents were there.

Together, with Raeburn keeping pressure on the wound, they splashed their way to the beach. Each of them helped carry Stuke across the hot sand, until they could lay him gently in the back of Dr. Doyle's truck. Emmet ran and gathered up Apollo, and everyone piled into the truck bed. Dr. Geaux started the engine and whipped open her phone, dialing while Dr. Doyle and the others worked on Stuke.

Dr. Doyle peeled off his T-shirt and handed it to Raeburn while he cradled Stuke's head in his lap.

"Raeburn, keep pressure on it with the cloth. Calvin, I need you to kneel at his feet. We're going to gently lift his leg and set it on your shoulder. We need to keep his foot elevated," Dr. Doyle said.

"It hurts! It hurts!" Stuke cried out. Riley gripped his hand in hers. Emmet took the other one.

"Hang on, buddy," Emmet said. "We're going to be at the hospital soon." Emmet kept talking calmly to Stuke as the truck zoomed over the road.

Dr. Doyle checked his eyes. "He's going into shock."

Emmet shook his hand. "Hey, Stuke! Come on, man. School starts in two weeks. You don't want to miss that! Tater tots in the cafeteria! Homework! Hang in there, dude. We're almost there."

Stuke continued to moan, tears streaming down his face. Apollo wormed his way into the crowd around the wounded boy and gently licked the tears away, as if comforting him in the only way he knew how.

A few minutes later, the truck screeched to a halt at the ER entrance of a nearby hospital. A trauma team burst through the door, and several orderlies lifted Stuke onto a gurney. The six of them watched in exhausted silence as they wheeled him inside.

The hot dogs were left forgotten and burning on the grill.

8

EVERYONE PACED NERVOUSLY IN THE WAITING ROOM adjacent to the ER. While doctors worked on Stuke, a nurse helped Raeburn get cleaned up and gave Dr. Doyle some scrubs to change into. All of them were still in swimsuits and vests. The kids were barefoot, having kicked off their swim fins on the beach. Dr. Doyle's and Dr. Geaux's clothes were soaked. They hadn't paused to gather up anything other than Apollo.

Now that Emmet had a chance to think about it, he was really proud of his dad. Dr. Doyle was an outdoorsman. Even though Emmet always made fun of him, calling him the Bird Nerd, his father was experienced at a lot of things. In Montana he'd been part of search-and-rescue teams that went into the mountains to find lost hikers and campers. First aid and triage were second nature to him, and he'd kept them all calm while they got Stuke to the hospital.

While they waited, the group huddled in the waiting room to discuss what had just occurred.

"What happened out there?" Dr. Geaux asked. Emmet and Riley were still a little too shaken up to talk, so Raeburn spoke up.

"Some kind of giant eels swam up on the reef from the deeper water offshore. One of them attacked Stuke. But I don't think it was an eel exactly. It *looked* like one, but it was bigger than any I've ever seen. It had a mouth shaped more like a barracuda's, and it could swim really fast," she said.

"Did it have any other unusual markings or colorations that you can remember?" Dr. Geaux asked.

"It had bluish-gray scales, and it was spotted along the gills, like some morays I've seen," Calvin said. "And . . ." He stopped, thinking, trying to recall details.

"What, Calvin?" Dr. Geaux prodded him.

"Like Raeburn said, they came out of the deep water offshore. And they headed straight toward the reef like laser beams. The weird thing is they ate the lionfish. Like they hadn't fed in weeks. We were swimming over the reef and there must have been a hundred lionfish there, maybe more. And those things, I think there were at least six of them, cleared that reef in minutes. I know a few other fish will eat lionfish if they're hungry enough, but they're not anything's first choice. But these things were like lionfish vacuum cleaners. It made me think of . . ." Calvin stopped.

"What is it?" Dr. Geaux asked.

"It's nothing," Calvin said.

Emmet looked at Calvin, then paced back and forth waving his arms around wildly. "You know it's not nothing. I tried to tell everyone, but nobody would believe me. I said he'd be back."

Dr. Doyle put his hand on Emmet's shoulder. "Emmet, we have no evidence that this is Dr. Catalyst's doing. Unlike land animals, it's not unknown for new species of sea creatures to be discovered. The ocean is a vast ecosystem that is home to —"

"Come on, Dad!" Emmet interrupted. "Who else would it be? I just learned less than an hour ago that the lionfish is an invasive species, exactly like the pythons and boas. The Pterogators appeared to take them out. Now, all of a sudden, this swimming dragon comes out of nowhere and starts chowing down on lionfish? And don't you think it's strange that it shows up right where we happen to be? What more evidence do you need? It's him. You know it's him. Dr. Catalyst is back!"

Dr. Geaux and Dr. Doyle exchanged uncomfortable glances. Dr. Geaux ran her hands through her short hair, like she often did when she was tired or nervous.

"Emmet, hon, I know how you feel about Dr. Catalyst. But we don't have a single shred of evidence he's involved here. And we need to find out more about what we're dealing with. I'll need to coordinate with NOAA and get a dive team out there. We need to photograph or capture one of those things so we can test —"

"Actually, Dr. Geaux," Riley spoke up, "I think I have all the pictures you need right here." She held up her right arm. Still dangling from her wrist was her underwater camera.

Emmet was thunderstruck. He'd been terrified, trying to find a way to get out of the water, and Riley had been playing crime-scene photographer.

"Seriously? You took pictures?" Emmet asked.

"Just at the beginning. When Calvin first spotted them. I thought they were weird looking. I didn't realize they were dangerous. After Stuke was attacked, I forgot I even had the camera. If it hadn't been for the wrist strap, I probably would have dropped it."

She handed the camera to Dr. Geaux.

"Riley." Dr. Geaux smiled. "You may have just given us a giant head start. I'm going to get these looked at. And then we'll figure things out. But now I have to ask all of you . . . given what we went through at the park the last time, let's keep any Dr. Catalyst talk to ourselves. Agreed?"

Each of them nodded in agreement.

But a few seconds later, they no longer needed to remain silent. A television running in the corner of the ER broke in with a news flash. A blond woman sitting at an anchor desk spoke with a grim expression

"Channel Five News has just received a new video from a person claiming to be Dr. Catalyst. South Floridians will remember him from earlier this year. Dr. Catalyst, as he called himself, was an environmentalist and geneticist that some are calling an ecological hero, but others a terrorist. According to authorities he was presumed dead, after releasing a fearsome new species of alligator in the Everglades and kidnapping a respected avian biologist. In this most recent statement, the person claiming to be Dr. Catalyst says he has unleashed a new hybrid species aimed at ridding the coastal reefs of the invasive lionfish, which have decimated the ecosystem. Dr. Catalyst warns that his new 'creation' lives only in salt water but is fast, aggressive, and should not be approached. He also says he plans to release more creatures soon, unless a set of forthcoming demands are met.

"Here at Channel Five News we must emphasize we cannot confirm the identity of the person claiming to be Dr. Catalyst, as Dr. Catalyst was declared missing by the FBI. We are working with our sources to learn if his status has changed. However, we have video of what *this* Dr. Catalyst claims are his newest hybrid creations. We must warn our viewers what you are about to see is graphic in nature."

And right there, on the TV in the ER, Stuke's friends watched again as he was attacked by something out of a nightmare.

9

DR. CATALYST WAS OVERJOYED. IF ANYTHING, THE resulting firestorm from the video he released overwhelmed even his earlier "media outreach" with the Pterogators. It was almost certainly a result of the attack on the Stukaczowski boy. (He had learned the name from the media reports.) Once again Emmet and Calvin had intervened, preventing his Muraecudas from killing the lad. Were they not thwarting him at every turn, he would admire their ingenuity. Their quick thinking had saved their friend from a more serious injury or even death.

Today he had emailed his South Florida Ecosystem Recovery Manifesto to every news outlet and environmental organization in the entire state of Florida. The response had been almost exactly as he expected. First, the local law enforcement agencies had formed a task force. They assumed he was using the Everglades as his base again.

But he crossed them up this time. Among his demands, he insisted hundreds of miles of coastline be shut down to public use, as well as the entire Everglades National Park. This would strain their resources. Additional rangers and other law-enforcement personnel would be gearing up to find him. Dr. Catalyst was presumed dead based on the blood evidence from his airboat recovered in their previous encounter, so at this point they were operating on the assumption that Dr. Catalyst had an accomplice in his hybridization efforts or that this new creature was the result of a copycat.

It made Dr. Catalyst laugh. As if any copycat could possibly hope to accomplish what he had done scientifically. A handful of others in the world might have the intellect or the resources, but they lacked the will.

It had taken so little effort to fool the idiots trying to catch him. Keeping a few pints of his own blood available was part of his standard contingency operation. Before he abandoned the boat, he spread it around the wreck to throw off the authorities. Apparently it had worked. Let them think there was another Dr. Catalyst at work. It gave him an advantage. This time he was hidden somewhere they would never look.

After losing his compound in the Everglades, he'd upgraded all of his data feeds. He now stored his information on computer servers at an offshore company that maintained the equipment and asked no questions as long as they received payment. It allowed him to use his tablet computer to keep track of all of his facilities and experiments. All of his labs were wired with motion-sensor cameras. If anyone showed up, he'd get a notification sent to his tablet and phone and see it right away.

With his fingers flying over his tablet, he checked on the tank holding a new batch of Muraecuda hatchlings. They were progressing rapidly and would be ready to release soon. All was going according to plan.

He punched another icon on the tablet and the screen split into several smaller screens showing the media broadcasts surrounding the environmental "crisis" he had created. Some stations where showing the video. Others were having roundtable discussions with so-called experts discussing what should be done to address the "Dr. Catalyst Problem."

Dr. Catalyst wasn't sure what triggered the thought. Perhaps it came from his plans to release his next batch of hybrids. Or it could have been from listening to the

politicians, environmentalists, and other windbags trying to figure out what he was doing or if he was even real.

He was real all right. And things were about to
become even more interesting for those who opposed
him. Dr. Catalyst was going to make things very real.

He was going to start a movement.

10

BEFORE THEY COULD DIGEST WHAT THEY HAD JUST SEEN, before Emmet could say "I told you so," a doctor finally emerged from the exam room. The group gathered in a half circle around him. The name on the pocket of his white coat read FLORES, and his sleeves had blood on them. Emmet tried not to think about it being Stuke's blood.

"We've managed to stop the bleeding," Dr. Flores said. "It's a vicious bite. We're going to have him airlifted to South Miami Hospital for surgery. He's stable and we've given him enough pain medication to knock him out. What is it that attacked him?"

Dr. Geaux stepped forward. "Dr. Flores, I'm Dr. Rosalita Geaux of the NPS and superintendent of Everglades

National Park. We're not quite sure what it was. It might have been a barracuda."

Dr. Flores shook his head. "I get a lot of injured swimmers in here. That's not like any barracuda bite I've ever seen. Whatever attacked the boy had a mouth full of teeth, but the bite pattern is not like —"

"I'll make sure the authorities are alerted, and we'll find out what happened," Dr. Geaux interrupted. "Right now we'd like to focus on Stuke."

Dr. Flores's eyebrows furrowed a moment. Emmet watched the exchange like it was a tennis match. He was almost ready to blurt out the truth but remembered his promise to keep the details secret for now.

"Hmm. Well, he's asleep now. We've also given him a huge dose of antibiotics to combat infection. The Life Lift chopper is inbound. If one or two of you would like to see him, you can wait with him until it gets here. That'll be fine. Now if you'll excuse me, I need to check on him again." Dr. Flores disappeared through the double doors back into the ward.

Emmet's dad and Riley went to check on Stuke, while Dr. Geaux made a call.

Before long, Emmet could hear the sound of the chopper approaching.

The drive to Miami seemed to take forever, even after Dr. Geaux called the Florida State Police for an escort to help them cut through traffic.

Stuke was in surgery when they arrived, but his parents were in the waiting room.

Stuke was an almost perfect combination of his mom and his dad. He had his mother's height and her round, friendly face. His dad had the same red hair and freckles, and was pacing intensely back and forth. Stuke's dad was a Florida City police lieutenant. He had already seen the footage on the television, and he was beyond angry, stalking back and forth in the waiting room, his body coiled. His jaw was so tight it looked like it had been carved out of granite. But he softened when he saw Emmet, Calvin, and the girls.

"You kids," Officer Stukaczowski said. "You saved my boy. My wife and I . . . we . . . the way you all took care of him . . . made sure he got to safety . . . we . . ." Tears formed in his eyes and he had to look away. His wife rubbed his shoulders and smiled at them, but she had teary eyes as well. Raeburn stepped up and gave him a hug.

"Officer Stukaczowski," she said, "it's okay. If it had been one of us, Stuke would have done the same thing."

He looked at Dr. Geaux. "When you want to start looking for this creep, I'm ready. My resources, contacts, sources, my off-duty hours — whatever you need, you've got it."

"Tom," Dr. Geaux said, "you know we're going to catch this guy. But don't worry about it now. Right now, let's be here for Stuke. We can think about Dr. Catalyst later."

Stuke was in the operating room for six hours, but the surgery was deemed a success. Even so, his recovery and physical therapy were going to take several months, and he would have to spend a few days in the hospital. The doctors wanted to dose him with antibiotics to make sure he didn't end up with an infection. The long, ragged bite on his leg had over one hundred stitches in it. It would probably leave a winding, jagged scar along the calf and knee of his right leg. Two of the tendons in his leg had been severed, but the surgeries had reattached them. Thankfully the creature hadn't broken any bones or permanently damaged any nerves. It was going to hurt for a while, and Stuke would be confined to a wheelchair while the stitches healed. But the main thing was he was going to be okay.

Emmet decided he liked Stuke's dad. He welcomed any new members to the "I Hate Dr. Catalyst" club. And it was probably a good thing to have a policeman on the membership roster.

But Emmet was still the president.

11

BY THE TIME SCHOOL STARTED, DR. CATALYST'S MANIFESTO was all over the news. It became such a big deal in the media that Stuke's dad came to the first day of school to talk about safety. He urged all the students to stay away from the beaches and to avoid the Everglades for the time being. Pterogators were still on the loose in the Glades and were driving the regular alligators out of the swamp and into more populated areas. The normal gators were getting hungry and desperate, and that made them more aggressive. He wanted everyone to be aware.

Dr. Catalyst called his new hybrids Muraecudas. They looked like someone had duct-taped the head of a barracuda to a moray eel's body and then added an extra serving of teeth. Nobody knew how many of these giant killing machines were out there, lurking in the ocean. The local authorities were not going to officially close the beaches. They were not going to give Dr. Catalyst the satisfaction. But Stuke's dad told everyone it was probably best to exercise caution.

Dr. Catalyst's manifesto, if it *was* Dr. Catalyst, had a list of demands a mile long. Emmet hadn't even read the manifesto because he'd heard it all before: Close everything. Someday I'll be thought of as a genius. Kick everyone out of the Everglades. I'm not crazy, I'm a visionary, and blah, blah, blah. There was a lot of other stuff in there about environmental policy and legislative initiatives that generally made Emmet's eyes glaze over.

Since Emmet had no intention of ever going back into the water under any circumstances, his mind drifted while the first-day assembly dragged on. As he fidgeted in his seat, his eyes wandered across the gymnasium and settled on Dr. Newton. He was standing with the rest of the faculty, along the gym wall. Still in his ratty tweed sport coat and his Birkenstocks. Emmet's eyes narrowed as he studied him. "Hey, Calvin," he whispered.

Unlike Emmet, Calvin was paying attention to every word Stuke's dad said. That Calvin was a stickler for rules.

"What?" Calvin hissed, annoyed. After the crisis with Stuke had passed, he had returned to his post-reservation-visit moodiness.

"Why is the Newt here? I thought he got suspended or put on leave or something."

Dr. Newton was Emmet's science teacher when he first came to Tasker Middle School last spring. Apparently he came from a wealthy family and had a PhD in biology, but had decided to devote his life to teaching. He was also an environmental activist who donated large amounts of money to preservation groups. When Dr. Catalyst had first emerged with his Pterogators, Dr. Newton had sort of taken his side in the media — even when Emmet's dad was kidnapped. Emmet was furious at the time. Dr. Newton believed all methods of ridding the Everglades of invasive species should be considered. Even Dr. Catalyst's. And he had said so publicly.

"Is he still on Dr. Catalyst's side?" Emmet asked him quietly.

"I don't know. My mom had him questioned by the FBI, but she said he didn't know anything. But I heard a lot of parents complained about him being on TV, saying so much stuff about Dr. Catalyst. The school put him on leave for the rest of the semester until things blew over. He shouldn't have said what he did, especially after what happened to your dad. I know you don't like him because of that, but he's still a good teacher. The school just decided that things should cool down. That's the rumor, anyway," Calvin said. "I guess with Dr. Catalyst gone they decided he could come back."

"Yeah, except he's not gone," Emmet said.

Calvin shrugged.

Emmet thought about this. After he and Calvin had rescued his dad from the swamp, Emmet had spent a week or so staying with him in the hospital and then at home while he recovered. When Emmet came back to school, Dr. Newton had already been placed on leave. Emmet had nearly forgotten all about him.

"Why are you so curious about the Newt, anyway?" Calvin asked.

"Oh, no particular reason," Emmet said. "Other than he's standing there acting like it's just another ordinary first day of school."

"Um. Because it is?" Calvin said.

"Yes," Emmet said. "But he doesn't usually have his right arm in a sling."

"Huh," Calvin said.

Emmet stood and moved past Calvin to make his way down the bleacher steps.

"Where are you going?" Calvin hissed.

"To ask him a question," Emmet said.

"Wait! What question? Emmet, hold on," Calvin said.

As Emmet started down the steps the assembly ended and students rushed out of the bleachers and onto the gymnasium floor, milling about before heading to their classes. Emmet kept his eye on Dr. Newton, who was now engaged in a conversation with a couple of the faculty members.

He was jostled by the crowd and had to dart around and through the masses.

"Emmet!" he heard Calvin calling behind him.

Emmet couldn't see over everyone, but he thought Dr. Newton was moving toward the gymnasium door. It didn't matter. Emmet knew where he was going. And as he caught glimpses of Dr. Newton through the crowd, his anger started to boil. He felt a little rush. It was good to have a suspect. He wished he'd thought to bring Stuke's dad with him so he could arrest Dr. Newton on the spot.

Leaving the gym, he headed past the cafeteria to where the hallway ended in a T, and turned left, heading for the science lab. Like a lot of schools, Tasker Middle School was designed with very little imagination. From the air it would look like a giant H, with the gym and the cafeteria in the middle part and the science rooms at one end of the parallel hallways.

Emmet was walking fast, barely acknowledging the "hello's" he received from teachers who stood outside their classrooms with clipboards, taking attendance for their first-day classes. Dr. Newton's classroom was at the very end of the hallway, across from Ms. Susskind's room, the science teacher he'd been switched to last semester. Emmet liked Ms. Susskind. She wasn't a no-good, dirty, ecoterrorist father-napper.

Dr. Newton stood outside his room holding a clipboard in the same hand that was suspended by the sling. Probably the very arm that was nearly bitten in two by a Pterogator. *Ha!* Emmet thought. *Serves him right.* His hair looked like it usually did, all curly and frazzled as if he'd just grabbed hold of a downed power line. As students filed by him into the classroom, Dr. Newton checked their names off on his clipboard.

Emmet stopped right in front of him. Dr. Newton paused and looked up from his list. Emmet watched his face very closely. At first confusion, then curiosity, followed by . . . Emmet wasn't sure. One of the things he had learned since his mom died was that a lot of times people said one thing but the looks on their faces said something else. People who hardly knew him would tell him things like, "Oh, Emmet, I'm really sorry about your mom." But when he looked at their faces, he realized they weren't all that sorry. Not really. They were just trying to be polite.

Emmet didn't know all the ways adults lied about things. He only knew that they did. But if he had to guess, he would have said the emotion that crossed over Dr. Newton's face right then was surprise with maybe a tad bit of fear mixed in. Dr. Newton wouldn't have to guess what Emmet was feeling because he had his mad face on.

"Emmet. Why, hello. How are . . . I didn't expect . . . I don't think I have you in my class this year, do I? How was your summer?"

"Hot," Emmet said. "What happened to your arm?"

"My arm? Oh. I was in a car accident."

Emmet studied the arm up close. The sling hid most of it, but he could see it was encased in a cast. It would be difficult to determine if the arm had been bitten.

"When?" Emmet demanded.

"When what?"

"When were you in a car accident?"

"I . . . uh . . . it was back in the spring."

"Really? That long ago? What happened?"

"What happened? Nothing, really. I was pulling into my garage, and I hit the side of the garage door hard enough for the air bag to go off. It broke my arm," Dr. Newton said.

"That's a long time for you to be in a cast, isn't it? Bones usually heal faster than that, don't they? I mean, it's a whole new school year." Emmet was really angry now. He didn't think Dr. Newton had a broken arm at all.

"I . . . A long time? I don't know. The doctor said it was a freak accident. I broke both bones so it has to be in a cast a little longer. At least, that's what I'm told."

Emmet squinted and stared hard at Dr. Newton. The whole story sounded like a convenient alibi. But Emmet had to be careful. Not everyone knew a Pterogator had attacked Dr. Catalyst. That detail had been kept secret.

"How is your dad doing, Emmet?" Dr. Newton asked. "I heard about what happ —"

It was a simple question. Even a polite one. And Emmet's parents had always raised him to treat people with respect and to use good manners. But this question? Coming from Dr. Newton? It nearly sent him over the edge. Turning red, he pointed his finger at the startled man's face.

"Don't you *ever* ask me about my dad," Emmet said.

He spun on his heel and stomped back down the hallway.

12

SOMETIMES YOU JUST HAD TO LAUGH. DR. CATALYST was doing that now. The reason clichés become clichés is because there is usually some measure of truth in them. And in this case the accuracy of that old saying "the best place to hide something is in plain sight" was proving itself beautifully.

Unlike his Pterogators, which were developed and hatched primarily in the swamp, his Muraecudas presented a far more difficult challenge. They could not live in freshwater. Thus the Everglades were off-limits, at least temporarily. He needed power, a filtration system for his saltwater tanks, and isolation. In the swamp, hiding was not a problem. It must have been pure dumb luck that Emmet and Calvin discovered where he was hiding Dr. Doyle. In fact, it ate at him a little bit. Maybe he would have a face-to-face talk with Emmet Doyle and find out what he knew. And teach the impertinent little twerp a lesson at the same time. But that would have to wait for later.

Dr. Catalyst had scouted several locations and facilities to serve as a base for his Muraecuda work. He couldn't risk someone stumbling upon his lab and finding out what he was doing by accident. One wrong turn by a tourist in a rental car, or a group of teenage vandals sneaking into one of his buildings, and everything would come crashing down.

His solution was another stroke of brilliance. On the outskirts of Florida City, a few miles west of Highway 1, was a long-abandoned amusement park known as Undersea Land. About forty years ago, a local entrepreneur tried to create a miniature ocean-themed attraction for the thousands of visitors heading to the South Florida beaches. Everything had a nautical theme. The merry-go-round allowed children to ride on the backs of plastic dolphins and whales instead of horses. Flying pirate ships replaced big-eared elephants.

The entire enterprise had been a huge flop. It barely lasted two years before the investors lost everything and closed it down.

But one of the attractions had been a live dolphin show. Inside a small, enclosed auditorium, dolphins and seals would perform tricks for the underwhelmed guests. It was a surprise to anyone visiting that the park had lasted as long as it did.

But it was perfect for his needs. The aquarium, once the equipment was upgraded and the tanks were filled with salt water, was the ideal place for him to produce his Muraecudas. His only problem was avoiding discovery. And he had solved it by going legitimate.

He created a series of shell companies and hired a developer, Mr. David LeMaire. LeMaire was the unsuspecting stooge in Dr. Catalyst's investment to refurbish and reopen a newer, better Undersea Land attraction.

LeMaire never met Dr. Catalyst, except via email and voice mail. This was not unusual. All over Florida there were plenty of real-estate developers who would do any deal anonymously, as long as the money showed up in their bank accounts.

LeMaire filed the permits, bought the property, and sent out a press release. He supervised the beginnings of the repairs and improvements, the most important of which was the construction of a nearly impenetrable twelve-foot-high solid steel fence around the entire park.

Shortly after the fence was completed and the aquarium refurbished, LeMaire received an email from Dr. Catalyst. Work on the renovation of the park was to cease. The crews were to be sent home. A problem with the financing had arisen and the new construction would have to wait. David LeMaire received his last bank transfer and went on to his next job with no questions asked. Real-estate deals fell through all the time in Florida. The newer, better Undersea Land was just another victim of poor financial planning, and soon it was forgotten. Again.

But the fence remained. And the refurbished aquarium no longer stood empty. It was where Dr. Catalyst was raising his newest species. Close to the ocean. Someplace no one would ever think to look.

Tonight he stood in front of the tank, watching his Muraecudas feed. They truly were magnificent creatures. Swimming, eating, killing machines, who devoured the lionfish he provided for them every day.

Unlike his Pterogators, these creations were not as . . . pliable. He could not teach them to seek out a specific prey as easily as he had done with Hammer and Nails and their clones. But he had chosen the exact right combination of aggressive reef-dwelling species. And lionfish lived and fed on the reefs. Well . . . his experiment had worked out better than he could have planned. By feeding them only lionfish, with each successive generation of clones, he was teaching their primitive brains to seek out lionfish as their first, preferred food source. Once in the ocean they would undoubtedly consume other species. They were predators, after all.

But they would consume vast quantities of the invasive species first, and help restore balance to the ocean.

Dr. Catalyst looked at the newspaper in his hand. The headline read GOVERNOR SAYS NO TO DR. CATALYST. FLORIDA'S BEACHES TO REMAIN OPEN. He tossed the paper away. They had not acceded to his demands.

It was time to up the stakes.

Dr. Catalyst opened the digital recorder app on his tablet computer. Pushing the record button, he began speaking. "Attention, people of South Florida. I am asking all of you who truly love our environment to join me in my quest. . . ."

13

IT HAD NEVER BEEN THIS WINDY IN THE TREE HOUSE
before. Calvin and Emmet were doing homework
there, as was their habit, after checking in with Mrs.
Clawson, the Geauxs' next-door neighbor. Apollo
stayed at the Geauxs' during the day, and Emmet usually took him for a walk after school. After that they
did homework or, if they didn't have any, played video
games or sometimes took their books up into the tree
house and studied there.

Dr. Doyle had Emmet coming here with Calvin most
days since school started. Emmet wasn't sure, but he
thought it had something to do with the fact that his
dad and Dr. Geaux were having so many dinners
together. In fact, they usually came home from work

64

together, and then the four of them would all eat as a group, either at one of their homes or at a restaurant. Emmet didn't really have time or even want to think about that yet.

Calvin didn't seem to mind him coming over so much. Of course Calvin probably wouldn't mind if a hoard of rampaging Vikings captured him and pulled out his toenails. Emmet was sure if that happened Calvin would just shrug and say, "They'll grow back." Calvin was slowly getting back to normal at school. At lunch he sat at the table with Emmet, Riley, and Raeburn, and sometimes he even participated in the conversation. And it was Calvin who politely kept anyone else from sitting in Stuke's seat until he returned to school.

Apollo didn't like the tree house much. They hadn't figured out a way to safely get him up to their lair. While they were up above he barked and whined and tried to climb up the trunk, until he decided to punish them by ignoring their existence. He would curl up beneath the tree and sleep until they came down. Even if they could get him up safely, knowing Apollo, he would leap through the screen as soon as he saw a bird. Apollo was not aware of his limitations. Especially the one about dogs not being able to fly.

Emmet had become very fond of Calvin's little hideaway. Somehow, being up above the ground with the tree gently swaying, he gained a little freedom and clarity. Except when he was mad about something. Like today.

"Is this thing safe in this wind?" Emmet asked. The boards were creaking and the branches were really swaying.

"Yes," Calvin answered.

"Are you sure?"

"Yes."

"Did you file the proper building permits?"

"Yes," Calvin said, not looking up from his math homework.

He was about to say "Seriously?" but then Emmet remembered he was talking with Calvin. Calvin filed a flight plan with the FAA if he made a paper airplane.

"Dude, what is going on?" Emmet asked.

"What? Nothing," Calvin said. He looked up from his math homework with a sour look.

"I don't want to get all up in your business, but ever since you came back from visiting your family, you've been a little . . ."

"A little what?"

"Morose. We did vocab in language arts today, third hour. *Morose* was on the list," Emmet said.

"What's *morose*? We didn't do that vocab yet."

"Gloomy."

"I'm not gloomy."

"No. You're more fun than a platter of bacon."

"Do you always have to make a joke out of every-thing?" Calvin sighed.

"Yes. It's my thing. We've discussed this. But I'm sorry. I just thought maybe something was bothering you. I'm all ready to go into a full-fledged rant, but you don't seem like you're in the mood. So I thought we'd have an Oprah moment and see if you've got something you want to get off your chest."

Calvin flipped over onto his back and looked up at the roof of the tree house.

"Sorry if I've been morose," he said. Emmet waited, but he didn't say anything else.

"It's okay. I just figured you got into some kind of family thing or something. My grandparents and my cousins live a long way away and I never saw them that much, anyway, but my mom and dad were always talk-ing about 'family drama.' People get worked up over that stuff."

"It's not that," Calvin said. "It's just . . . You can't tell anyone this . . . especially my mom. She'd get all upset. And she has enough on her plate."

"Calvin, I promise, not a word to anyone. Not even your mom. Unless you're going to run away and join the circus or something. That's never a good idea." Emmet grimaced because he couldn't help himself sometimes. He made a mental note to rein it in. Soon.

"I turn thirteen next year," Calvin said. "In the old

days it was different, and now each tribal group does things their own way, but in our clan, when a Seminole boy turns thirteen, there's a ceremony where you are given your name. It's . . . Usually your father picks it, and there's a feast and stuff. And . . ."

"And your dad won't be there," Emmet said, understanding.

"Right," Calvin said quietly.

"Calvin — and this is a serious question — what do you mean, 'given your name'? Don't you already have one? I don't understand."

"*Calvin* is my legal name. When you are a Seminole you can have several names during your life. Most of the old warriors' and chiefs' names could and did change based on their accomplishments, or things they did to benefit the tribe. If they won a great battle or defeated a mighty enemy, for instance. But your first real Seminole name is usually given when you're around thirteen. And it's chosen by your father."

"All right. I get it," Emmet said. "But here is another real question. I'm not a big history buff or anything, but I know the Seminoles and most American Indians got treated pretty badly. I'm talking about disease and wars and stuff. So there must have been other Seminole boys who didn't have fathers when it was time for this ceremony. Can't a relative stand in? A grandparent or an uncle?"

"Yeah. My grandfather died, and my dad was an only child. One of my great-uncles probably will. But it won't be the same," Calvin said.

"No, it won't," Emmet said. "Not ever."

A few moments of silence passed, and then Calvin asked, "What did you want to rant about?"

"What? Oh, that. It's nothing, really," Emmet said.

"It's okay. I don't feel morose anymore. Actually, an Emmet rant would sound pretty good right about now."

"I might not stop, once I get started," Emmet warned.

"Do you ever?"

"Hah! You should do stand-up. Like stand up and walk away," Emmet said.

"You're going to tell me anyway, though, right?" Calvin asked.

"Of course. It's about Dr. Newton," Emmet said.

14

DR. NEWTON'S CONFRONTATION WITH EMMET DOYLE had rattled him. All day he watched the clock, let his classes essentially run wild, and kept willing the hours to move faster. When the last bell finally rang, he let out a huge sigh of relief. He herded the last student out the door to his classroom and shut it, leaving himself alone. Fishing his phone from his pocket, he placed a call. Someone picked up after two rings, but there was no greeting. This is how the calls always went.

"There is a problem," he said into the phone. "We need to meet. The usual place in ninety minutes." The person on the other end never spoke, did not make a sound of any kind. The call was disconnected, and he stuffed the phone back into his pocket and grabbed his battered briefcase.

"If they only knew," he muttered. Dr. Newton burst out of the room and scurried down the hallway, making a beeline for his car in the faculty parking lot. It took him a little longer to open the doors and get seated inside with only one good arm. After the accident he had purchased a new Lexus. These displays of wealth were all part of the plan.

His drive through the Florida City streets was cautious and deliberate. The traffic was light, but he drove just below the speed limit, checked his mirror carefully, and doubled back several times to be sure he wasn't being followed. Dr. Newton was nothing if not careful.

Finally, he maneuvered the car through a mostly empty industrial park and came to a stop at an underpass beneath the freeway. He removed a small pair of binoculars from his briefcase and quickly scanned the surrounding area. There was no sign of surveillance, or of anyone watching.

Five minutes later a large black sedan pulled up next to the Lexus. The tinted windows obscured the driver. Dr. Newton lowered his window all the way, but the other driver only cracked theirs slightly. Just enough to hear what Dr. Newton had to say.

"Emmet Doyle might be a problem," Dr. Newton said.

"Define *problem*," the other driver replied.

"He confronted me in school today. Asked about my arm. He was . . . angry," Dr. Newton said.

"And how is this a problem?" the mysterious driver asked.

"You don't understand. He's smart and . . . determined. If he starts nosing around —"

"*If* he starts nosing around," the driver interrupted, "we will take action. Until then, keep an eye on him. If it seems like he's putting his nose where it doesn't belong . . . remove it."

"No. You aren't hearing me. This could ruin everything. Taking his father changed the dynamic. It could lead to —"

The driver interrupted. "We're talking about a twelve-year-old. I don't see why this is a problem, and I don't understand why you felt the need to tell me this in person. *That* can ruin everything. Keep an eye on the kid. Remember how much time and effort we have invested here. Don't mess this up."

The driver's window rose into place with a *click*. In a few seconds the car was gone. Dr. Newton watched until it vanished from sight, then drove to his home. Along the way he was doubly cautious. Checking his rearview mirror, studying the side streets, and looking for anything suspicious. He saw nothing.

When he arrived at his home, he pulled into the garage. This time he did not hit the door.

15

CALVIN'S TREE HOUSE CAME EQUIPPED WITH A SMALL radio. The boys used it to listen to music while they were doing homework. Just as Emmet was about to launch into his rant, the music on the radio stopped, and a voice cut in with a news bulletin. At first Emmet was prepared to ignore it, but when the announcer mentioned Dr. Catalyst, he stopped. Calvin turned the radio up just in time to hear a recording of the world's biggest lunatic playing over the airwaves.

". . . and all citizens of South Florida. Your misguided and guilty politicians have refused to close the beaches. As a result, you leave me no other choice. You have seen the video of what my creatures can do to a swimmer. As of tonight, several dozen more Muraecudas will be released at multiple locations all around the South Florida coast. I cannot guarantee the safety of anyone who enters the water. Do so at your own risk. This action demonstrates my seriousness in this matter. You have been warned." His voice was disguised by one of those electronic voice synthesizers, which made him sound like a robot.

"People of Earth . . ." Emmet muttered. "What a loon."

The announcer cut back in, saying that several media outlets had received the recording from the individual claiming to be Dr. Catalyst. They would have more details as soon as they became available. Now, back to our regularly scheduled programming.

"Hmm," Calvin said.

"What? What's 'hmm' mean?" Emmet asked.

"It's weird," Calvin said.

Emmet was sitting crisscross applesauce on the floor of the tree house, and he put his head in his hands. Having a conversation with Calvin was like waiting for paint to dry.

"What's weird? And please elaborate. Feel free to use more than one- or two-word answers in your responses."

"I just don't get why he wants to make such a big show of it. If you're going to open up a new critter-in-the-box to save the environment and stop invasive species like he claims, why go to the media? Wouldn't it be better to release your creatures into the ecosystem on the sly and then have scientists and all the agencies running around, bumping into one another, trying to figure things out?"

Emmet stared at Calvin in openmouthed wonder.

"What?" Calvin asked

"That was awesome," Emmet said.

"Quit it," Calvin complained.

"I just think Dr. Catalyst — who is Dr. Newton, by the way — wants the attention."

"He's not Dr. Newton," Calvin said. "We've already been through this."

"How do you explain the broken arm?"

"How did *he* explain the broken arm?" Calvin asked.

"What do you mean?" Emmet was squinting at Calvin now.

Calvin snorted. "Emmet, everybody knows you got in Dr. Newton's face. It was all over school in about ten minutes."

Emmet hadn't considered that. Angry as he was, he barely remembered getting to his first-hour class. But he did remember angrily shouting at Dr. Newton.

"His story about the car accident stinks," said Emmet.

"Maybe he did have one," Calvin offered.

"It's too convenient. He's my number-one suspect," Emmet said.

"He's not a suspect," Calvin said. "Remember, my mom had him questioned by the FBI. There was nothing there. Believe me, my mom likes Dr. Newton about as much as Apollo likes fleas. Nothing would give her greater satisfaction than slapping him in cuffs and dragging him off to jail. Especially after what happened to your dad. But it's not him."

Emmet stared off into space. He still thought Dr. Newton was up to something. If Emmet had his chance, he'd like to give him a little interrogation of his own.

His thoughts were interrupted by the sound of Dr. Geaux's car pulling into the driveway, followed closely by his dad in the pickup. Dr. Newton's interrogation would have to wait — at least until after dinner.

16

THE BOAT SLICED THROUGH THE WATER OF MODEL LANDS Basin. Dusk was approaching, and the coming darkness would help disguise his activities. Dr. Catalyst piloted the craft with precision, circling in a widening arc until most of the other boats had left. To an observer he looked like any other fisherman.

He let the engines idle until the boat glided to a stop. For the last three nights a large pontoon boat had brought divers to this area, offering patrons a chance to snorkel the reef at night. Dr. Catalyst could hardly believe their stupidity. Apparently they didn't know that most species of sharks fed at night. It never ceased to amaze him how casually some people behaved toward nature. Another reason why the environment was being ruined: careless behavior.

The group there tonight was about to get a visit from creatures that were very hungry and would be attracted to the noise and lights of the divers. Not to mention the fact that the reef was crawling with lionfish.

Dr. Catalyst opened the catch tank. With the flashlight app on his tablet he inspected his Muraecudas. There were six of them today. He watched as they slithered and splashed in the shallow water. It was feeding time.

Pressing an icon on his tablet was all it took to release the creatures into the ocean. The mechanism whirred and the cover folded into place. The stern of the boat sank slightly as the tank took on water, but then righted itself as the bottom closed and the pump siphoned the now-empty tank. Even if he'd wanted to stop his creatures, he couldn't.

Now he waited. Though they were fast swimmers, it would take some time for his beasts to cover the distance. And unlike with his Pterogators, he was unable to attach a camera or tracking device to these creatures that would survive the extended exposure to salt water. He would know they'd reached their destination by the reaction of the swimmers.

He waited at the stern, watching. As the minutes passed and nothing happened, his spirits flagged. Something must have gone wrong. The Muraecudas might have been distracted by a school of fish, or found something else edible between his boat and the divers. The resistance of this species to training had proven more problematic than —

Shouts echoed across the water. First the voices sounded curious. As if someone aboard the pontoon boat was attempting to clarify something. Then came yells of alarm, rising in pitch and frequency. Apparently the divers had just been introduced to South Florida's newest predator.

Dr. Catalyst scanned the boat with his night-vision binoculars. People were clambering out of the water. Two of the divers were clearly injured and had to be dragged aboard by the others. Their screams were the loudest of all.

There was a great deal of commotion on the deck. Dr. Catalyst couldn't see the state of the injured divers, but the boat's engines started up, and it accelerated quickly across the water. Even over the sound of the engines, he could still hear the agonized screams of grown men in horrific pain. Someone shouted, "More pressure! You need to apply more pressure!" followed by, "We've got to stop the bleeding!" and he smirked. They had learned a cruel, hard lesson.

He watched until its running lights disappeared as it approached the shore.

Dr. Catalyst set the night-vision goggles on the console of his boat and slid the throttle back. His vessel picked up speed, and he carefully navigated a return course to his base. Hopefully the divers would report their encounter to the authorities and the media would run with it. After that it was up to the governor, Dr. Geaux, and the rest of the government toadies.

Until then, he would continue to escalate tensions. He would release more and more of his Muraecudas until someone blinked. In the meantime, he had one more thing to do that would really create attention for his cause.

Turning the boat, he headed north. He had urgent business in Florida City.

17

THE NEWS OF THE ATTACK ON THE DIVE BOAT WAS ALL over the school the next day. One diver had lost three fingers on his left hand, and another had his arm crushed by a thunderous bite from one of the Muraecudas. The man would need to undergo several operations to regain even limited use of his arm. Both had nearly bled to death before they reached the emergency room. Now the gossip and buzz in the media and throughout the entire South Florida area was whether or not the state or local government was going to close the beaches. Dr. Catalyst was not giving them much of a choice.

At lunch, Riley and Raeburn were talking about nothing else. Stuke was still recovering at home and they all missed him. In fact, Calvin would still politely ask other kids not to sit in "Stuke's spot" at their table, and all of the students honored his request. His seat would remain empty until Stuke returned to fill it.

Emmet thought about how they'd seen these beasts up close. Reliving their experience was not fun, yet they did it. All of his friends had a theory on the true identity of Dr. Catalyst.

Emmet wished he could tell them about Dr. Newton. Or his "Dr. Newton obsession," as Calvin called it. No one knew about Dr. Catalyst's arm injury. Dr. Geaux had told them they couldn't say anything about it. Of course, you could dump a truckload of bricks on Calvin and he wouldn't say anything. Emmet was nearly bursting with an intense need to spill his guts.

As the group talked on, Emmet kept shooting Calvin looks. Calvin kept staring back at him like . . . Calvin. Emmet wondered what type of news would provoke him to do more than slightly raise his eyebrows. Believing — knowing — that Dr. Newton was Dr. Catalyst was killing him. Finally, Emmet couldn't take it anymore. He had to do something.

There was still a half hour of lunch left when he made an excuse about having to study for a history quiz. He told everyone he was headed for the library. After dumping his lunch remnants in the trash, he headed to his locker, wanting to grab his backpack to be ready for the first bell. When he closed his locker door, Calvin was suddenly standing there.

"Dude!" Emmet yelped. "Quit sneaking up on me!" Emmet startled easily.

"I'm not sneaking. I'm standing," Calvin said.

"What do you want?"

"You don't have a history quiz."

"I do. . . . You don't have my . . . history . . . How do you know what quizzes I have?" Emmet stammered, though it wouldn't surprise him if Calvin knew the schedule of every student in the school.

"Raeburn is in your history class. She said you don't have a quiz this week."

"Yeah, well, I still need to study. So, see ya. I'll catch up after school." He started down the hall.

"Don't do it, Emmet," Calvin called after him.

Emmet stopped in his tracks. A few other kids walked by, and he waited until they passed before answering.

"Do what?" he asked.

"I know what you're up to, bro."

"Okay. Here's a tip. Don't say *bro*. It's not you. And you know that I'm 'up to' what, exactly? Studying history?"

"No. It's lunch hour. The teachers are in the staff lounge. You're going to go check if he's there and if he is, you're going to see if his room is open and search for clues."

"What? Pfft! That's crazy talk. No, I'm not."

"Yes, you are, Emmet. And you're going to get in trouble." The way he said it made it sound like poking around a teacher's empty classroom was a capital offense. Calvin walked up close to Emmet and lowered his voice.

"Emmet, you're wrong. But just for a minute, say you're right. Dr. Newton is really Dr. Catalyst, evil genius. Okay, he's got the money and resources, and a PhD in evolutionary biology. He's all over the news and on all these boards and stuff, and is all about saving the environment."

"You see! Not so crazy now, is it?" Emmet said. Only the more Calvin talked, the crazier it sounded.

"Yes, it is. But suppose all of this is true, and Dr. Newton really is Dr. Catalyst. Do you really think he's going to leave clues lying around his classroom?"

"Calvin, I don't know. But Dr. Catalyst has to be caught. Your mom is working nonstop on the task force, and my dad is stuck in the swamp all day still trying to round up his CrazyGators, so they don't have time to look for clues. And no one else has any idea where to start. I've got to do something. You don't have to be involved, but I've got to do something."

"How can I help?" Calvin said.

"In fact, you can just pretend like you didn't even . . . What did you say?"

"What do you need me to do?"

Emmet was unprepared for Calvin to give in. At best, he hoped Calvin would just agree not to get in his way or turn him in.

"I'm sorry. I thought you said you'd help me."

"I did."

"Why?"

Calvin shrugged.

"And now we're back to the shrug." Emmet sighed. "Come on. Follow me."

Emmet's locker was around the corner from the gym. They headed down the short hall, and Emmet slowed as they passed the staff lounge. Pausing for a few seconds, he heard Dr. Newton's voice mixed in among the other teachers'. He sped up again until he was past the lounge and then stopped. Calvin was right behind him.

"You have your phone?" Emmet asked him. Ever since Dr. Catalyst had taken his dad prisoner, Dr. Geaux had given them each a special park-service phone. Technically they weren't allowed to have phones in school, but they did.

"Yeah."

"Is it charged?"

Calvin frowned. Emmet realized he'd said the wrong thing. Calvin kept everything neat and orderly. The president of the United States was more likely to accidently leave the nuclear launch codes in the restroom at

McDonald's than Calvin was to have his phone anything less than fully charged.

"Of course you do. You wait here at the intersection of the hallway. If Dr. Newton comes out of the staff lounge, text me."

Emmet started down the hallway. He looked back to see Calvin standing there, his hands at his sides, stiff as a board. His very posture would tell any teacher or administrator who walked by that he was up to something.

"For Pete's sake, loosen up," Emmet hissed.

Calvin tried leaning casually against the wall. He then adjusted himself and tried it again, this time with one leg propped up behind him. Then he switched and crossed his arms and tried leaning against the wall. Next, to Emmet's horror, he put one hand on his hip and the other on the wall and tried it that way, but no matter how his arms and legs flailed around, he still looked suspicious. Emmet shook his head. Poor Calvin. It was a little like watching a baby moose doing yoga.

With everyone still at lunch the hallway was mostly empty. This time, though, it seemed like a much longer journey to Dr. Newton's room. The door was closed. Emmet took a deep breath. Any potentially dangerous chemicals for the science classes were stored separately — they didn't allow middle-school kids to make anything more hazardous than mold — but Emmet was still surprised to find the door to the room was unlocked. He opened it a crack. "Hello?" You could never tell with the Newt. He might have someone on room detention during lunch hour. The Newt was a stickler for discipline. No one answered. So far so good.

Emmet went straight to Dr. Newton's desk. It had three drawers on one side and a single long drawer under the desktop. Emmet pulled the long drawer open first. Nothing but pencils, staples, and other office supplies. The other three drawers were crammed full of homework assignments, more office supplies, and a jar with a preserved frog in it. But so far nothing incriminating. No hidden recipes for Pterogators. No journals labeled SECRET FILES OF DR. CATALYST or CONFESSIONS OF AN ECOTERRORIST.

Emmet pounded his fist on the desk in frustration. He looked around the room. There had to be something. On top of a cabinet on the wall near the desk he spotted a battered briefcase.

It was old and beat-up, the leather scratched and torn, with simple latches rather than a combination lock. Emmet's heart sank a little. Calvin was right. It was unlikely Dr. Newton was going to leave anything here that would prove he had a secret identity as a crazed, animal-inventing criminal.

The briefcase held a tablet computer, some homework assignments, a small pair of binoculars, and a folded-up newspaper. Emmet was about to close it when he spotted a green file folder buried under all the stuff. He pulled it out and looked inside. He found a bunch of newspaper clippings about the Dr. Catalyst incidents. It included computer printouts of articles about alligators, barracudas, great gray owls, DNA research, vampire bats, and a Miami Dolphins schedule.

Apparently Dr. *Newtalyst* was an ecoterrorist football fan. And Emmet had just found his scrapbook.

Right as he was about to stuff the file in his backpack, Emmet felt his cell phone vibrate in his jeans pocket.

He'd just received a text.

18

DR. CATALYST WAS MAKING THE FINAL PREPARATIONS at the aquarium. If everything went according to plan, the tide would finally turn. This next act would show the world how far he was willing to go. It would also strike a blow against Dr. Geaux and Dr. Doyle. After this, they would realize he was not to be trifled with. And they would leave him alone to complete his work.

The tank in the aquarium was buzzing with Muraecudas. Unlike the Pterogators, they required fewer hormones to accelerate their growth. They achieved full size and length in a matter of weeks. Swimming about in the backlit tank, they were fearsome to look at. Their long, undulating bodies and blunt faces filled with dozens of spear-shaped teeth made them look just as fearsome as their Pterogator brethren. The bodies were made for swimming hard and fast through the water, devouring whatever crossed their paths.

As they swam and circled the tank, some of them would occasionally surge toward him, bumping their heads hard against the glass when he wandered too close. They were ready to eat him, were it not for the barrier.

Dr. Catalyst used a large wrench to attach the final connector to an electronic winch bolted to the aquarium. Cable fed out of the winch to a pulley system on the ceiling. Hanging suspended above the open water tank was a steel cage. The sight of it dangling a few feet above the water was chilling even to him. Depending on what happened in the next few minutes, he would know whether or not he would be required to use it.

The governor's next press conference was scheduled to begin momentarily. Dr. Catalyst punched a few buttons on his tablet and brought up a live Internet feed. There on a stage stood the governor, a tall, thin man dressed in a gray pinstriped suit. His hair was flecked with gray at the temples, and his face looked a little sunburned, as if he'd just been called in off the golf course. Behind him were gathered several mayors from South Florida cities, police officers, and FBI agents. He even saw Dr. Geaux in her park-service uniform among the toadies assembled there.

"Good afternoon," the governor said. "I will make my remarks brief. I'm here to announce the expansion of our joint task force consisting of personnel and resources from several state, federal, and local agencies. This task force's objective is twofold. First, to reverse the environmental damage being done to the state by the release of artificially enhanced species by the criminal calling himself Dr. Catalyst. Appropriate state and federal agencies will coordinate efforts to capture and destroy these animals before the harm they are causing becomes irreversible. Second, the task force will also use the law-enforcement capabilities of these combined agencies to locate and apprehend the fugitive calling himself Dr. Catalyst by any means necessary.

"Because of her scientific training, as well as the law-enforcement experience she brings to this job as the superintendent of one of America's foremost national parks, I am asking Dr. Rosalita Geaux to serve as task-force director. Her efforts thus far have resulted in the safe removal of dozens of hybrid creatures from the Everglades. She has accepted these additional duties with my thanks, as well as the personal thanks of the secretary of the interior.

"I will say one final thing before Dr. Geaux takes your questions. We will not close the beaches. We will not close the Everglades. Though the park is federal property, I have the word of the president of the United States on this. Dr. Catalyst will not dictate policy to this state or any municipality. Our beaches will remain open. We do ask people to exercise caution, as these species are dangerous and unpredictable. But we will not allow a terrorist to dictate how we live our lives.

"I also ask the public's help in this. Be vigilant. Report any suspicious behavior or activity, as it is unlikely a single person would be able to effectively carry out an operation of this size. It is very likely he has help, so watch for suspicious boats or individuals, or anything that appears out of the ordinary. Together we can bring an end to Dr. Catalyst and his misguided and malevolent schemes. That is all I have to say. Dr. Geaux will be taking your questions now."

His rage building, Dr. Catalyst watched as Dr. Geaux approached the microphone. Reporters shouted questions, but his vision had turned red and his hearing dimmed to the point where he couldn't concentrate on anything being said. Something about twenty-four-hour hotlines being established. Environmental teams dispatched to control the creatures. Extra beach and swamp patrols. It was all just white noise to him.

The governor had called him a terrorist. A terrorist! "Unlikely to be working alone," he had said, as if he were some imbecile! The governor, who allowed the environment in his own state to be flushed down the drain, was calling *him* a criminal! What a tin-pot, small-minded, bought-and-paid-for, self-important fool!

Dr. Catalyst stomped back and forth in front of the tank, attempting to walk off his anger. He kneaded his mangled hand hard against his thigh. He would have punched something, had he not feared damage to his remaining working arm. It took several slow, gasping, deep breaths before the raw emotions receded.

If he was to succeed, he must not let these fools stop him. Looking up at the cage, he pushed a button on his tablet and the winch motor whirred, lowering it a few feet closer to the tank's surface. He pushed another button and the cage floor, hinged along one side, swung open. Inside was an open container of lionfish. It splashed into the water and the Muraecudas immediately converged, devouring them in a matter of seconds.

His little device worked perfectly.

Terrorist. He would show them a terrorist.

The tablet held a map program, and he pulled up one of the marshes and inland waterways in nearby Florida City. The Aerojet Canal ran right behind the Doyle residence. With a little maneuvering he could reach it from his boat.

It was time to raise the stakes.

19

HIS PHONE BUZZED AGAIN. PULLING IT FROM HIS POCKET, the screen lit up with Calvin's message: *9-1-1.* The file was in his hand. It was evidence. Of something. He didn't know what to do.

If he took the file, Dr. Newton would notice it was gone and it might spook him. He could go underground. They might never find him. If he didn't take it, he'd have no way of convincing Dr. Geaux or his dad that Dr. Newton was at least up to something. And if he stood around trying to figure out what to do much longer, Dr. Newton would catch him in his room, and he didn't have an excuse ready. But if he took it and the Newt found out, he might be putting everyone in danger. The only way to prove anything was to take it.

He glanced at the file again. Then he remembered Dr. Newton's desk drawers. They were full of folders, old homework assignments, tests, and other assorted junk. Maybe he could pull a switcheroo. Now was his chance.

Emmet put the file in his backpack. He opened the middle desk drawer and found an empty green folder. Grabbing a handful of papers of approximately the same thickness, he jammed them into the folder and replaced it in the briefcase. Maybe Dr. Newton didn't look through it every day. Emmet could only hope. He scurried to the door.

There was nowhere for him to go except out in the hall, and if he barged out of the room now, Dr. Newton might see him. Emmet slowly opened the door, holding his breath and just hoping the hinges didn't squeak. If his quarry were heading this way, he would be spotted for sure.

His cell phone came with a camera. The viewfinder was in the front corner, but the view screen was in the back. Emmet held the camera so only the small hole for the viewfinder went past the doorframe. It took a bit of adjusting, but he managed to maneuver it so that he could see Calvin and Dr. Newton standing at the intersection of the hallway.

Calvin had positioned himself so the teacher had his back to Emmet as they talked. Emmet couldn't quite hear what they were saying, but it was an animated conversation. Calvin was moving his hands around a lot more than usual, maybe to keep Dr. Newton's attention.

Emmet stepped into the hallway and quietly shut the door behind him. Then he saw the flaw in his plan. Calvin couldn't keep Dr. Newton talking forever, and there was no place for Emmet to hide between the room and where they were standing.

Ms. Susskind's room was across the hall, so he hurried over and tried it, but the door was locked. The other classrooms in the hallway were all too close to Dr. Newton.

Emmet was stuck. No place to run. No place to hide. No restroom. Not even a janitor's closet. There was only one direction to go: forward. As he started down the hall toward them, he saw Calvin's eyes widen slightly. For Calvin this passed as an expression of great alarm.

"Do you think they swim in schools, or do you think they are more solitary like the moray eel?" Emmet heard Dr. Newton ask Calvin.

Calvin was staring right at Emmet, and his eyes widened another three millimeters. Dr. Newton didn't notice.

"What?" Calvin said. "Oh. I don't know. There were five or six of them, so a school, I guess. But Stuke was bitten, and we had to do the swimming. And there was a lot of blood. Then he was screaming. Stuke, I mean. Not the fish thing. And I had a snorkel."

"I see," Dr. Newton said, sounding confused.

Emmet was cringing. If Calvin were ever forced to turn to a life of crime, he needed to make sure he was *never* captured. He would last about three seconds in an interrogation.

The conversation was winding down. Any moment Dr. Newton was going to turn around and spot him.

Emmet spied the bulletin board a few yards away. It was covered with posters, announcements, and flyers. He stole toward it as quickly as he dared, slipping a pencil and a scrap of paper from his backpack and pretending to be very interested in copying down information about an upcoming fund-raiser for the school band.

The bell rang, and the surge of students emerging from the lunchroom could be heard through the whole building. Dr. Newton and Calvin's conversation was drowned out by the rising noise. From the corner of his eye, Emmet saw Dr. Newton bid Calvin good-bye and turn toward his room. He stopped when he discovered Emmet in the hallway.

Emmet finished writing down his pretend information and stuffed the scrap of paper into his backpack. He looked up, making direct eye contact with Dr. Newton.

"Mr. Doyle," Dr. Newton said with a small measure of surprise in his voice. "I didn't see you there."

Emmet looked at him, trying to give the hardest stare his twelve-year-old face could muster.

"I saw *you*," Emmet said. He was pretty sure Dr. Newton's face reddened a little bit.

He slung his backpack over his shoulder and walked toward Calvin, who was still waiting at the intersection of the hallway. He didn't break eye contact with Dr. Newton the whole way.

"How's the arm?" he asked.

Dr. Newton narrowed his eyes at Emmet. Without a word, he turned and hurried to his classroom.

20

THE CONTENTS OF THE FILE WERE SPREAD OUT ON THE floor of the tree house. Emmet stared at them like a voodoo priest might study a pile of bones. There was something in all of this. What it was, he hadn't quite figured out yet.

Calvin was sprawled on a beanbag in the corner, nearly catatonic. His body was stiff, and his legs and arms were splayed out to his sides like a turtle on its back. He stared at the ceiling of the tree house without blinking.

"I'm never doing that again," he said.

"I hope not," Emmet said.

"What? What's that mean?" Calvin lifted his head.

"It means you su — . . . are not very . . ." Emmet caught himself. "We all have different gifts. And being sneaky is just . . . not in your nature," Emmet said. Carefully.

"Yeah, well, so I'm not a ninja like you. We almost got caught breaking the rules," Calvin said.

"Relax, we weren't holding up a bank," Emmet said.

"You took someone's personal property."

"It's called evidence."

"Evidence? Of what? That Dr. Newton is a Dolphins fan?"

"He's involved in this somehow."

"You don't know that," Calvin said. He groaned and sat up.

"Why would he have all this stuff?" Emmet said. "It'd be one thing if it was just news clippings, but there's other stuff here. Information from a lot of different scientific websites about the creatures we've encountered, and some we haven't yet. And while we're on that subject, I hope we never do. Vampire bats? I hate bats."

"Actually, bats are pretty harmless and really useful to the environment."

"You are a walking nature documentary, do you know that?"

"Yes. Emmet, the real question is — what are you going to do with that file?"

Now it was Emmet's turn to flop backward on a beanbag. Throwing an arm over his eyes, he tried to think. The governor had expanded and enlarged the Catch the Environmental Supervillain Task Force, and Calvin's mom was in charge of it. Now even busier, she'd asked his dad to take complete charge of Pterogator removal in the Everglades and help her find some experts on the new creatures. The upshot was both of their parents were more occupied than ever.

By all rights he should give the file to Dr. Geaux and have her deal with it. Of course this would bring up the very uncomfortable question of how he came to acquire it. In her mind, Dr. Newton had been questioned and cleared. She probably wouldn't be overjoyed that Emmet had recently taken up cat burglary. His dad definitely wouldn't like it. And since Emmet didn't exactly have a warrant to search through Dr. Newton's private stuff, who knows if they'd even be able to use it.

"I don't know," Emmet said. "Yet. I need to think on it."

"Just don't ever ask me to do that again, bro," Calvin said. "I'm still a little freaked out."

"We've discussed the *bro* thing," Emmet said, his arm still over his eyes.

The sound of their parents' cars arriving moved them both to action. There was no way Calvin would ever allow him to hide the file here. That would be a big, giant screaming bag of no-no as far as Calvin was concerned. Emmet stuffed the file in his backpack, and they hustled down to greet their parents.

Apollo had already run on ahead and was getting his nightly dose of affection from Dr. Geaux.

"Hey, boys," she said.

"Guys," Dr. Doyle chimed in. Both of their parents looked really, really tired. Like dead-on-their-feet exhausted.

"Emmet, if you've got all your stuff, we're just going to head home and pick up some takeout along the way. I'm beat. Going to hit the sack early. That okay?" Dr. Doyle asked.

"Sure, Dad, anything is fine," Emmet said.

They said their good-byes and climbed into the truck. On the way, they grabbed burgers and shakes, and an extra burger for Apollo, who was not pleased when he discovered that burgers disappear when you eat them. Emmet thought that Apollo divided his days into thirds: looking for food, eating the food he found, and then getting ready to look for even more food. Wrapped around periods of sleep. A short while later, they arrived home.

Dr. Doyle stumbled off to bed, muttering, "Good night." Emmet had homework and spread out on the kitchen table working away, with Apollo sleeping at his feet. Emmet usually tried to do well in school and took his homework seriously. Before long he looked up and realized it was almost time for bed.

Apollo rose and walked to the back door, scratching at it. He waited for Emmet to open it to begin his nightly perimeter check. The back door of their house opened out to a fenced-in yard, with three cypress trees dotted throughout it. Behind the yard was a canal, and so any home with outdoor pets had to have a secure fence to keep the alligators out. Of course this didn't prevent the little black mutt from smelling nearby gators and barking his head off.

Emmet cleaned up the kitchen and repacked his books in his backpack, ignoring the green file that was still there. Until he figured out his next step, his plan was to pretend it didn't exist. At least until morning.

Emmet wasn't sure how much time had passed with Apollo outside. Apollo sometimes became fixated on a leaf or a bird feather that might have floated into the yard. It often took upward of half an hour to thoroughly smell whatever delicacy he may have uncovered.

While brushing his teeth, he thought Apollo made a funny noise from outside. Not a bark of fear or pain, but a strange *yip*. Emmet rinsed his mouth and went to the back door. When he flipped the switch beside it, two powerful outdoor floodlights snapped on. His dad had gotten them installed after Dr. Catalyst had kidnapped him. The lights were powerful enough to illuminate every corner of the backyard.

"Apollo?" Emmet called. He stepped through the door onto the small concrete slab that served as a patio. There was no answering bark. Apollo usually appeared whenever Emmet called him. "Apollo?" he called again.

His eyes traveled to every corner of the yard. He didn't see the dog anywhere.

But he heard something.

In the darkness beyond the fence, down in the canal, a powerful boat engine roared to life. Emmet had been in Florida long enough to know the sound of the throttle being engaged and heard the propellers churn through the water. He sprinted toward the fence as fast as his legs would carry him, not thinking of any danger that may lie in the blackness beyond it. He leapt and pulled himself to the fence top in time to see the running lights of a boat headed south, disappearing around a bend of the canal.

"APOLLO!" he shouted.

21

DR. CATALYST WAS SPEAKING OUT LOUD TO HIMSELF, rehearsing for the next recording he would soon release to the media. The boat was docked in the river that ran right past Undersea Land. He had carried the dog inside. He believed it was named Apollo, if he remembered correctly from the audio recordings from his bugs at NPS headquarters. It was stirring now, the effects of the tranquilizer beginning to wear off.

The cage trap now rested on the concrete. Dr. Catalyst opened a small door on the side and placed the dog on a blanket he had laid on the bottom.

With his tablet he activated the winch, and the cage rose in the air. Another touch and it swung over the tank until it hung suspended, ten feet above the swimming creatures.

"I am not a monster," Dr. Catalyst said to the empty aquarium. "I am no criminal. It is not I, nor the creatures I have created, who have damaged our environment to the point of no repair. In my quest for change I have used controversial methods. But it has never been my intention to harm anyone." He paced back and forth, repeating the lines over and over. In one of his previous media statements, he had asked for the public to join him. His hope had been for his supporters to get in the way of the authorities. But so far, only a few fringe environmental groups had offered token support. He was sure it was because he was being unfairly portrayed by the media.

"There is a saying that desperate times call for desperate measures. I have made my conditions clear: Close the Everglades to the public. Cease all efforts to reclaim the Pterogators from the park. Close all beaches, and allow my newest species to clear the reefs of the destructive lionfish. If that does not happen by ten A.M. tomorrow, the automated timer above this tank will open the floor of the cage. I do not need to provide the graphic details of what will happen next. I ask the members of the media to use restraint in showing this video to children. It was not my wish to take this drastic step, but I have been given no choice. Ten A.M. tomorrow."

When he was ready, he activated the wireless video cameras. The split screens showed a view from the cage floor into the tank below. The water was a foamy mass of swirling fins, tails, and teeth. A longer view showed Apollo, who had come groggily to his feet. Still dazed, he was sniffing around this strange new enclosure. A third shot, at an angle, showed the cage hanging above the tank. Apollo was clearly visible inside it.

After recording several minutes of video, Dr. Catalyst finally pushed the audio-record button and recited his comments. Once completed, he replayed them. The program allowed him to overlay the audio with the video images of Apollo in the cage and the Muraecudas swimming below him.

When the video was done to his satisfaction, he emailed it to his list of media contacts, including Dr. Geaux's personal NPS address. There was no way it could be traced back to him.

He activated the winch and lowered the cage safely to the ground beside the tank. There was no reason to leave the pooch suspended there. Unlikely as it was, something could happen to the mechanism, and there was no need for an unnecessary accident.

Apollo barked louder, growling low in his throat as Dr. Catalyst approached the cage.

"Easy, boy," he said calmly. "It's all right. I've got a nice, cozy room for you to stay in. Food, water, a bone."

His words had no effect. Apollo was angry. Snarling and snapping now any time Dr. Catalyst squatted next to the cage and reached for the latch on the door. It was almost amusing, he thought, the amount of indignation such a small creature could show. As the dog seemed to calm for a moment, he lifted the latch and opened the door.

An explosive, ink-black ball of angry fur catapulted out of the cage and a mouthful of sharp teeth sank into Dr. Catalyst's injured hand. He screamed and stood, trying to free himself, but the dog's grip was unbreakable.

He shouted in pain and dropped his tablet. It bounced and clattered on the ground. With his free hand he clawed at the dog's jaws, desperately trying to get loose, but Apollo was committed and would not let go. Waves of agony cascaded up his arm.

"LET GO!" he bellowed. To his complete surprise, Apollo did just that, dropping the short distance to the ground, landing deftly on his feet. He darted quickly behind Dr. Catalyst and sank his jaws into the calf muscle of his right leg.

Dr. Catalyst howled and danced and shook, but no matter what he tried, he couldn't break free.

"Ow! OW!" he shouted again, but he was in an awkward position and finally tripped over his own feet, tumbling to the ground and striking his forehead on the hard cement floor. Dr. Catalyst didn't believe his day could get much worse, but it did. Apollo let go and backed away, crouched and growling.

What the doctor did not know is that when Apollo was a puppy and Emmet was a little boy, Apollo's favorite game in the world wasn't fetch, it was "grab and go." Emmet would throw a ball or a stick, and instead of returning it, Apollo would entice his young master to pursue him through the yard or field.

The trouble was Apollo enjoyed playing "grab and go" at the worst times, with the most inconvenient objects. Anything in the house that fell to the floor was fair game. Apollo would snatch it up with his jaws and be off like the wind.

As Apollo spotted Dr. Catalyst's tablet computer now lying on the floor, the old game kicked in. He grabbed the tablet in his jaws.

And he went.

22

EMMET FELT WEAK. HIS DAD CAME STAGGERING OUT OF the house at the sound of his shouts, still half-asleep. Emmet yelled for him to get the truck and try to follow the boat by road, but his dad first stumbled around the yard, making sure there wasn't a hole in the fence that Apollo had dug under somewhere.

By the time they were in the truck and speeding along the streets paralleling the canal, there was no sign of the boat.

As they drove back toward their house, Dr. Doyle called the police on his cell phone. He put it on speaker so he could call hands-free.

"This is 9-1-1. What is the nature of your emergency?" the operator said.

"I need to report a stolen dog," Dr. Doyle said.

"Sir, this is an emergency line," the voice on the other end of the phone said. "Do you have an actual emergency?"

"Yes, it's an actual emergency! Dr. Catalyst stole our dog! Now get the police to put out an APB on —" Emmet shouted.

"Who is speaking?" the operator asked. "This is a line for emergencies only. If you need to contact the police department for nonemergencies, that number is —"

"Shut up!" Emmet yelled. Apollo being gone was starting to make him feel stunned and helpless, and he didn't like it. Not one bit. "Dr. Catalyst stole our dog. His name is Apollo. He's a black —"

The operator cut him off. "Young man, if you're playing a prank, there are very serious consequences for that."

Dr. Doyle clicked off the phone.

"Dad!" Emmet yelled at him.

"Hold on, son," Dr. Doyle said. He punched another button on the phone. It rang twice, and then a very sleepy Dr. Geaux answered.

"Hello?" Except to Emmet it sounded like "Smello."

"Rosalita? It's Benton. Sorry to bother you, but we might have a problem."

"Dr. Geaux! Dr. Catalyst took Apollo!" Emmet shouted.

Dr. Geaux was awake now. And her voice came through the cell phone loud and clear.

"Tell me what happened," she said.

Emmet repeated the details of the last few minutes.

"All right. Go home. I'm going to get the task force on this. I'll get the Coast Guard to bottle up the river so no boat can get through from the canals to the bay. Emmet, I'm going to need you to think about the boat. I realize it was dark, but how big was it? How many lights did it have? Was anything about the size or shape unusual? I know it's hard, but try to remember anything that might help. I need to hang up now. I'll be at your house in twenty minutes."

The truck bounced through the streets. Emmet begged his dad into following the canal one more time, but they didn't see anything. After fifteen minutes more of fruitless searching, Dr. Doyle turned the truck around and they sped home.

Emmet didn't know what to do. Part of him felt like crying. Another part of him felt like punching something. When they finally reached their street, there were two police cars in front of their house. Dr. Geaux arrived almost simultaneously with them. One of the police officers was Stuke's dad, who had gotten himself assigned to the task force. Dr. Geaux huddled with them for a minute or two, then one of the cars sped off.

The other remained behind to keep watch while the three adults and Emmet went inside.

"Emmet," Dr. Geaux, said, "I understand how worried you must be. You know how much I love Apollo. But I've got to ask you again, so Officer Stukaczowski hears it as well. Please tell us exactly what happened."

Emmet did, telling them about doing his homework, letting Apollo outside, and the strange yelp he made.

"Did he sound hurt?" Lieutenant Stukaczowski asked.

Emmet thought for a minute. "No. Once he got his paw caught in the screen door at our old house, and he squealed. He makes a different sound if something hurts him. This was like he was . . . surprised. I didn't . . . I should have . . . If I'd gone outside right then . . ." Emmet couldn't help it. Tears were starting to form in his eyes. Stukaczowski put his hand on Emmet's shoulder.

"Emmet, you listen to me. You didn't do anything wrong. If it was this creep claiming to be Dr. Catalyst, and I'm betting it was, we're dealing with a nut job. What you're describing sounds like your dog was sedated. Our Animal Control officers use tranquilizer guns, and when a dog is shot with one it often startles them. They make a little yelp, and they go to sleep. This is good news. It means whoever took Apollo, your dog's probably okay. You didn't hear a gunshot, so my guess is he's keeping him to force us to do something."

"Like what?" Emmet asked.

"I don't know yet," Lieutenant Stukaczowski said. "But I'm pretty sure we'll know soon. In the meantime, I want you to look at something." Using his phone, he pulled up a screen that showed the silhouettes of several different types of boats. Handing it to Emmet, he said, "Can you scroll through these and tell which one most closely resembles the boat you saw?"

Emmet looked through the images and found one matching the shape of the boat he'd seen in the canal.

Lieutenant Stukaczowski took it back from him, a puzzled expression on his face. "A fishing boat? Why would he be using a fishing boat?"

"Maybe to blend in," Dr. Geaux said. "Think about it. He's not in the Everglades. His airboat was a lot easier to hide out there. If he uses a really fast or fancy boat right now, it might call unwanted attention. One of the smaller commercial fishing craft . . . it might be slower, but nobody is going to pay attention to it. And he's probably modified it, boosted the engine with all his high-tech gizmos.

"Whoever this is —" Dr. Geaux went on.

"It's him," Emmet interrupted her.

"Emmet, I know your opinion, but we've talked about this. The blood we found at the accident site . . .

it's likely the real Dr. Catalyst had an accomplice, or someone who's taking up his cause. A fanatic who went to that much trouble, dealing with such dangerous creatures, would have someone to take over in case something happened —"

"It's him!" Emmet shouted.

The adults in the room went silent. Dr. Geaux looked down at the floor.

"Emmet," his dad said, "I know you're upset. And I want Apollo back, too. But you don't need to speak —"

"Why doesn't anyone believe me?" he shouted. "I was there! I looked into his eyes! So did Calvin! If it were me running around like this loon, doing all this crazy stuff, I'd have a plan in place to make it look like I'd died if I needed to get away. Haven't any of you ever been to the movies? The criminal always fakes his death!"

"Emmet, I'm sorry, hon," Dr. Geaux said. "But . . ."

Emmet would hear no more of it. Without another word he stormed away to his room and slammed the door. Inside he threw himself onto his bed. He couldn't stop the tears. It felt like he was losing everything. First his mom, then Montana, and now Apollo.

When he had finally cried himself out, he sat at his desk and plugged in his laptop. He went to his school website and looked at the staff listings. After all this time, he didn't even know Dr. Newton's first name.

Everyone just called him Dr. Newton or the Newt. In the staff directory he discovered it was Peter. A few more minutes searching *Florida City* and *Dr. Peter Newton* in a search engine gave him an address.

He could hear the adults talking in the room outside his door. They were giving him space. Emmet dug through his backpack and found some spare change and his city-bus pass. He stuffed them into the pockets of his cargo shorts, along with his cell phone and charger.

As quietly as possible, he lifted up his bedroom window, removed the screen, and slipped out into the night. He cut through the backyard of his next-door neighbors to avoid the police car in front of the house. Then, when he made it out onto the sidewalk, he started running.

He was going to pay a visit to Dr. Newton. Or should he call him Dr. Catalyst? Emmet wasn't sure, but he knew one thing.

He was getting his dog back.

23

DR. CATALYST LIFTED HIMSELF TO HIS KNEES. HIS HEAD hurt and his hand was bleeding. He reached back and felt the spot on his calf where he'd been bitten. His fingers came away with more blood on them. How had such a small dog done such damage? It felt as if a Rottweiler had attacked him.

There was no chance the dog could get out of the park. The fence surrounding it was twelve feet high. Still, he did not look forward to chasing it down. The mutt was apparently both vicious and devious.

As he climbed slowly to his feet, he looked around for his tablet. It was protected by a hard shell case, but he was using it to run his systems and needed to make sure it wasn't damaged. But he didn't see it. The first rows of bleacher seats in the aquarium were a few feet away. Perhaps it had tumbled beneath them. Groaning with the effort, he sank to his knees again and searched carefully beneath the metal benches.

The tablet was not there.

It was gone. Had the dog picked the tablet up and run off with it?

"Doggie?" he called to the darkened aquarium.

There was no sound. The noise from the pumps and filters powering the tank would have drowned out a response, anyway.

"Apollo? Here, boy!" he shouted again.

Nothing but silence.

He wasn't too concerned. All the doors leading into and out of the aquarium were closed and locked.

Still, hunting down the dog was going to be a waste of time, and he needed to get back to work. For that, he needed his tablet. He would go to the operations room, turn on all the lights in the building, and track down the dog.

An open doorway behind the tank led to a room filled with power switches and a console with equipment that controlled the pumps and filters. Dr. Catalyst flipped on the switches, and the room, as well as the rest of the aquarium, lit up in the harsh glow of fluorescent lights. Dr. Catalyst heard a soft *thump* and thought he felt a brief gust of air. He glanced beneath the equipment console as he made his way through the room. Even with the lights on, Apollo was completely black and would be difficult to see in the shadows.

Then the bumping sound again. And again. When he reached the end of the room he found the source. It was the door that entered from the outside. The door he used to get to and from the aquarium. The way he'd entered when he carried the unconscious dog inside a short while ago. Apparently it had not latched completely shut. Apollo was loose in the park.

Still Dr. Catalyst did not panic. Removing his phone from his pocket, he launched a GPS application that would track the location of the tablet. He had planned for every contingency.

On his phone's screen a blue map of the area appeared. He zoomed in until the map showed the park. In the center of the map a red dot was moving in a zigzag pattern. It was Apollo, running around wildly with his tablet.

Dr. Catalyst stepped through the door and into the darkness. This was only a setback. It would be time-consuming to track the dog down and retrieve both it and his computer. But he would have the dog back and inside his cage, suspended over the tank, in time for his next broadcast.

24

EMMET GOT OFF THE BUS AT THE STOP CLOSEST TO DR. Newton's address. According to his Internet search, the teacher lived on a cul-de-sac on the south side of the city. It made Emmet wonder for a moment. There was only one listing for a Dr. Peter Newton in Florida City in any of the online directories. But if Dr. Newton was so wealthy, why did he live in a tiny little house in a nondescript neighborhood? Wouldn't he have a ginormous mansion somewhere?

Emmet thought about this as he followed the map on his cell phone's screen. Newton was a fairly common name. Maybe there was another Peter Newton and the Newt's address just wasn't listed. Perhaps he didn't live here at all. As he continued, Emmet tried to talk himself back into it. Dr. Newton lived in a tiny house because it saved space. Stopping habitat destruction was a big part of the environmental movement.

It was about a ten-minute walk from the bus stop to the cul-de-sac. When he saw the house from the street, doubt crept in again. The place was pretty drab. If Dr. Newton was living here, he was really sacrificing for his various causes.

Emmet stuffed his cell phone away. He stopped on the sidewalk for a moment. For the first time, he felt a little nervous. This was the ideal hideout for a super-villain. Dark street. Not a lot of activity. Nothing behind the house but an empty field.

As he walked cautiously closer down the sidewalk, his eyes straining to see in the dark, he realized he'd made a mistake. It was eerily quiet in this neighborhood. If Dr. Newton really was Dr. Catalyst, he certainly wouldn't be storing his Muraecudas in a tiny three-bedroom house. And it was unlikely he'd brought Apollo here, either.

He stood on the sidewalk next to a large cypress tree, considering his options. Finally, he decided he'd come this far. There were no lights on in or outside the house. It was nearly pitch-black, and he hadn't thought to bring a flashlight. After a couple seconds he remembered his cell phone. It should give him enough light from the screen to see the ground in front of him, at least! As he pulled it out of his pocket, a hand reached out from behind him and touched him on the shoulder.

Despite himself Emmet gave out a bloodcurdling scream.

25

DR. CATALYST ZOOMED IN ON THE MAP ON HIS PHONE'S screen. It didn't show the surrounding area in great detail, but the little red dot was moving in the northwest corner of the park. That would place Apollo somewhere near the merry-go-round.

Once he retrieved the dog he would place it back in the cage. He still had enough time to take another group of hatchlings out to the sound and release them, returning before sunrise. Releasing them at night reduced his chances of getting caught.

By taking Apollo, he was forcing Dr. Geaux's hand. She had become close to the Doyles. Indeed he watched her on the surveillance tapes at the park, and it was clear she had become attached to the mutt. Dr. Catalyst looked at his bleeding hand, the red blood still visible in the darkness, and laughed. Apparently they were unaware Apollo had a dark side.

"Apollo!" he called. There was no response. In the engine room at the aquarium there was a small access closet, and that was where he intended to keep Apollo between filming sessions. He had grabbed some treats on his way out, and now he waved them about, hoping the dog would catch their scent. He slowed to a walk, and then stopped completely, concentrating on listening. The merry-go-round was up ahead, and he could faintly see the outlines of the plastic whales and dolphins on the now-decrepit contraption. The red dot on his screen was only going to give him a general location. Right now it was just a blip near the machine.

Up ahead he thought he heard something. A rustling sound, and maybe the slight jingling *clink* of a collar.

"Apollo?" he called, trying to make his voice sound as appealing as possible.

All was quiet. Slowly he advanced toward the merry-go-round, just a few more paces. Then he paused again, listening.

"Apollo?"

It was silent for a few seconds. He heard something behind the merry-go-round *clunk* onto the ground, then heard a scraping sound and a scurrying noise. He turned the corner, and there was Apollo, barely visible in the darkness. The dog dropped the tablet for a moment to rest, panting, but right as Dr. Catalyst extended his hand, the dog picked it up again and scurried away.

Checking his phone, Dr. Catalyst watch as the red dot moved on the screen, heading away from his current spot. He hurried along after the dog, cursing silently to himself.

This could take all night.

26

"**W**HOTHEHOLYGAHMCNARYIOUSWAHHH!" EMMET shouted. He couldn't help it. It was pitch-black on the street and someone had just reached out and grabbed him.

When his feet landed back on the ground, he remembered his karate lessons and took a defensive posture with his legs spread and his hands up. Now recovered from his shameful display, he was determined that Dr. Newton was not going to take him down without a fight.

A small flashlight clicked on, revealing Calvin.

"Did someone order a ninja?" Calvin said.

"Dude! Why do you keep trying to give me a heart attack?!" Emmet complained. Though he relaxed his posture, a small part of him was disappointed it was Calvin and not Dr. Newton. If it had been Dr. Newton, he at least could have demanded answers.

"What are you doing?" Emmet said. "Does your mom know you're here?"

"Does your dad?" Calvin countered.

"No fair. And I asked first."

"So we're back to being six again? No, my mom does not know I'm here. She told me what happened and called Mrs. Clawson to come over while I supposedly slept. Mrs. Clawson is nearly deaf. She had the TV volume up so loud there was no way she was ever going to hear me climb out my window. I hopped on the bus, and here I am," Calvin said.

"How did you know I'd come here?"

"Because you are so obvious."

"I'm not obvious."

"Emmet, you can't do this. What do you think is going to happen? Knock on the door, unmask Dr. Newton, and get Apollo back? It's dumb. You're not dumb."

"What would you do? I can't just sit there and wait. He's got Apollo. . . ." Emmet couldn't say the words.

Calvin didn't say anything. Not for several moments.

"Did I ever tell you about my ancestors? About the Seminole Way?"

"No."

"Back in the 1800s we fought the U.S. Army to a standstill for forty years. Made them spend millions of dollars. The tribal leaders did it by making the soldiers come to them, and by never fighting when or where or how the U.S. military expected."

"Calvin, I know this is important to you, but right now —"

"You didn't let me finish," Calvin said, holding up his hand. "There were only a few thousand Seminoles all together. And they fought a bigger, stronger foe to a draw. You did the same thing when you went and got your dad."

"What? I'm sorry. You lost me," Emmet said.

"Do you think Dr. Catalyst ever thought a couple of kids in a canoe would come and rescue Dr. Doyle? Did he think for even one minute you'd figure out where he was hiding or how he was doing it? Not in a million years. But you did it. So do it again."

"What? I just got lucky. He's not in the swamp this time. . . ."

"So figure out where he is. Tomorrow is Saturday. There's no school, so we can find him. You come up with something, and of course no one will listen to us, therefore we'll just skip the part where we try and convince anyone, and go right to saving Apollo."

"But this *was* my something. Dr. Newton is my only lead."

"We're going to go home. Get your dad to drop you off at my house in the morning. Then we'll figure out where Dr. Catalyst is and go get Apollo," Calvin said. He put his arm on Emmet's elbow and steered him down the street. A few minutes later they were back at the bus stop.

"Calvin?"

"Huh?"

"Why are you helping me this time? Last time you were all 'There's no way' and 'What if you're wrong?' and now you actually want to jump in with both feet. Why?"

Calvin shrugged. "I really don't like people who pick on dogs."

As Calvin and Emmet waited for the bus, they did not see the Lexus that had been shadowing them with its lights off ever since they left Dr. Newton's house. It pulled over to the curb and stopped. Inside the car, Dr. Newton punched a button on his steering wheel, and the phone connected after two rings.

"We've definitely got a problem," he said.

27

WHEN EMMET ARRIVED HOME, THE POLICE CAR WAS still in the street and Dr. Geaux was sitting in the kitchen talking to his dad. Lieutenant Stukaczowski must have left. Emmet went back in through the window, hoping and praying that they hadn't come in to check on him. He would be toast.

He changed into his pajamas, took a deep breath, and opened the door to the hallway leading to the kitchen. When he entered, both of them stopped talking and looked at him expectantly.

"Are you okay, hon?" Dr. Geaux asked. Emmet would never say anything, but he liked the way she called him "hon."

"Yeah. I couldn't sleep and came out to say I'm sorry. It's just . . ." He let his words trail off.

"It's okay, son," Dr. Doyle said. "But Rosalita has everyone out looking. We're going to get him back." Emmet could tell he was trying to sound confident.

"I know," Emmet said. "Dr. Geaux, if you don't find him tonight, in the morning would it be okay if Dad took me to your house, so I could hang out with Calvin? I like the tree house. It's relaxing up there."

"Of course," she said, standing. "Benton, I'm going to leave. Try and get some sleep, and then you can join the search teams tomorrow. You can bring Emmet by early. Mrs. Clawson will be there to keep an eye on them."

Hah! Emmet thought to himself. An entire column of tanks could drive down the road in front of Mrs. Clawson's house and if her game shows were on, she wouldn't notice. Best not to let them know that, though.

While his dad was busy saying good-bye to Dr. Geaux at the front door, Emmet went digging in the junk drawer by the phone in the kitchen. When they'd moved in a few months ago, they got a welcome packet from the Florida City Chamber of Commerce. Inside was a big folding road map of the entire area. He dug under all the other junk and grabbed the map, stuffing it in the waistband of his pajamas.

"You sure you're okay?" his dad asked when he came back into the kitchen.

"Yeah. I mean, I'm upset, but there isn't anything I can do. Dr. Geaux has her best people out searching. . . ."

His dad gave him a big, bone-crushing hug. Emmet had to admit it felt pretty great.

"I'm okay. Good night, Dad."

"Good night, Emmet."

As he reached his bedroom door, his dad called out, "Emmet?"

"Yeah?" Emmet said.

"I'll take you to Calvin's in the morning. But . . . I know what you did last time, and I know why you did it. You came and got me. It was brave. Dangerous, but brave. Sit this out, Emmet. This guy, whoever he is, is getting desperate. And that makes him unstable. Promise me you won't try to do anything."

Emmet thought hard for a way to answer without potentially breaking a promise to his dad. Unfortunately, he came up blank.

"Okay, Dad. Good night."

Emmet slipped into his room and shut the door. He took a red marker and his laptop from the desk, and sat cross-legged on the bed. Unfolding the map before him, he studied it long into the night.

28

IT WAS SEVEN A.M., AND EMMET AND CALVIN WERE IN the tree house. Emmet had brought the map, and he showed Calvin what his long night of research had revealed. He had narrowed Dr. Catalyst's base down to twelve possible locations. He figured that Dr. Catalyst was likely to have his lair on the mainland, and not one of the Keys or tiny islands dotting the coast.

"Why?" Calvin asked, when Emmet explained his idea. "Why wouldn't he go somewhere more remote? Like he did in the Everglades?"

"I thought about it a lot. There are plenty of reasons, but the most important are power and electricity. And salt water. He needs it for these creatures. If he's hatching them like he did the Pterogators, he'd need big aquarium tanks or a place right on the coast with a fenced-in pen full of salt water to keep them alive. He could have his own generators on an island, but what if they run out of gas or something? Say he's on the mainland doing Dr. Catalyst stuff and then a storm comes up. There are high waves. He can't get back, they run out of gas, and his creatures die. He's bold, but he wouldn't take a risk like that with his critters."

Calvin conceded the point. They didn't really have much choice. They couldn't get a boat out to the Keys, anyway.

"Second reason is, we found him last time and he had to escape. An island only gives you one way off. Unless he knows how to fly a helicopter or has a jet pack or something. Suppose someone else stumbles upon him this time? Then what? If he's on the mainland, he could have a boat or a car. Heck, he could even hide in the bushes, run back to the Everglades. There are a million places he could go."

"Good thinking," Calvin muttered as he peered over the map. But he said it in the Calvin way, so it sounded like he was praising a little kid for coloring inside the lines.

Calvin turned up the police scanner he'd brought up with them. Because of her job, Dr. Geaux had a home unit in case of storms or emergencies. Calvin had listened to it all morning. He set it on the floor beside them. All kinds of chatter came over the speaker from police and fire vehicles out on the road.

"These places here on the coast have already been searched," he said, running his fingers along the map. Two were abandoned fisheries and the other was a closed frozen-seafood warehouse. Calvin put an *X* over the circle Emmet had drawn around each one.

They both studied the map intently. There were now nine spots. Working together, they eliminated four more because of their locations. They were all close to busy streets or highways, which made it too easy to be spotted. Dr. Catalyst would have to move the creatures either by truck or by boat. Two of the places were on the river, so a boat was possible, but there were a lot of still-active businesses around them. Again, it was more likely someone behaving clandestinely would be discovered there.

"What about this place?" Emmet said, pointing to Undersea Land.

Calvin shook his head. "It's deserted enough, but there's no power. Been abandoned for years. It used to be a really cheesy amusement park. My mom took me there a couple of times, but it closed when I was, like, seven."

Emmet flopped back on the beanbag and put his hands over his eyes. He was exhausted. They'd already spent an hour trying to figure it out. The realization that he was going to lose his dog was starting to settle over him.

"Unless . . ." he heard Calvin say.

He sat up. "Unless what?"

Calvin was using his laptop. "A while ago, some rich developer bought it. He was going to upgrade and reopen the park. They started working on it, but I remember people saying the economy went bad and the guy lost all his funding or something."

"Why would it be an option for Dr. Catalyst if it's all old and moldy now?" Emmet asked.

"Well, I just thought of it when I saw it on the map. It had an aquarium for the dolphin-and-seal show. They weren't very well trained. But the tanks . . ."

Emmet sat up and snatched the computer from Calvin's hands. He searched and found a news article: "Undersea Land Redevelopment Loses Funding." He read it quickly, then looked at the park's location on the map. It was right by the river. It was very remote, which probably explained why it had failed the first time. The article said the "expected residential development nearby" never occurred.

Handing the map back to Calvin, he pulled up a website that let you look at a satellite image of any location in the world. Calvin read off the street number, and Emmet entered the address. A grainy image of Undersea

Land slowly appeared. Then the image cleared, and Emmet could see a roughly oval-shaped fence. Inside there were some paved walkways and a lot of roofs and buildings. At the southern edge of the park was a large rectangular structure, and there was a faded image of a dolphin painted on the roof. Emmet navigated in for a closer look. *It must be the aquarium*, he thought

It looked completely deserted, almost ghostly. Calvin scooted around so he could look.

"That's the place. Even the food was horrible. Nothing but seafood. How many kids like seafood? And if you were a kid visiting Undersea Land and you just saw Lucy the Lobster, Cubby the Clownfish — who was really creepy, as I recall — and Sammy the Shrimp on the midway, why would you go to one of the restaurants and order fish sticks and popcorn shrimp? No wonder the place failed. What's that?" Calvin pointed to the screen. "Right here. Outside this gate. Looks like tire tracks."

Emmet clicked the touch pad on the laptop and made the image larger. There were definitely tire tracks in the mud outside the fence.

"Doesn't mean anything," Emmet said, dejected. "They could have been there a long time."

"We haven't had any rain in a week or so. And look here," Calvin said, pointing.

In the upper right-hand corner was a box that revealed all kinds of information about the image. The latitude and longitude, and most importantly the date and time the image was photographed.

Two days ago.

29

INSIDE THE HOUSE, THEY EXPLAINED TO MRS. CLAWSON they were going to ride their bikes to the library to work on a school project. It was only a few blocks away, and they'd be back at lunchtime.

"That's just fine, boys," Mrs. Clawson said. Emmet thought her voice sounded like sandpaper. He had no idea how old she was. The Florida sun had baked her skin to the color of brown clay. She could be fifty or eighty. "It's so nice to see young people taking their schooling so seriously. Emmet, I do hope the police find your Apollo before that awful man harms that sweet puppy. I just saw on the news what he was doing. Poor Apollo. Those awful creatures! What would possess a man to do something like that?"

"I really don't know," Calvin said. "But going to the library will keep Emmet's mind off it. Come on, Emmet. Thanks, Mrs. Clawson."

Calvin herded Emmet toward the garage, where two mountain bikes were parked. One belonged to Dr. Geaux. It was pretty cool, even if it was teal. Emmet didn't care. He just wanted to find his dog.

"What was she talking about? Apollo and those 'awful creatures'?" Emmet asked him.

"I don't know. She's not all there half the time," Calvin said, pointing to his head. "I think game shows have rotted her brain. Let's ride."

Calvin picked up a backpack and ambled over to the tool bench in the back of the garage. He put some stuff inside, but Emmet couldn't see what it was. With Calvin, probably a miniature bulldozer or a bazooka. Calvin slung on the backpack, got on his bike, and left the garage before Emmet could ask any questions.

They had to wait for one of the bigger, articulated buses. In Florida City you could bring your bike on these double-size models. It was a city ordinance passed to promote health and wellness, and cut down on traffic. One of them stopped and opened its center door, and they carried their bikes aboard. It took forty-five minutes until they reached the southernmost stop, closest to Undersea Land.

Once off the bus, they wasted no time. Calvin pedaled so hard Emmet almost couldn't keep up. Only a few minutes later they arrived at the abandoned amusement park. It sat far back off the road, and the parking lots around it were now cracked and overgrown with weeds. The gigantic fence encircling the park made the place look like some derelict military camp. The place was kind of eerie, even in the daylight. Add the fact that Emmet was convinced Calvin knew something he wasn't telling, and Emmet's nervousness grew. He also knew trying to get Calvin to reveal something he didn't want to would take hours. They didn't have that kind of time.

They rode around the entire park looking for a way in. There wasn't one. The construction fence was solid steel and only had two entrances, both of them big enough to drive trucks and bulldozers through, but also currently chained and locked. The gates at the entrances were even more intimidating. They were composed of double doors with large metal brackets in the center. A thick chain ran through the brackets and was fastened with a large tempered-steel padlock. Emmet was getting a little weirded out. Something told him this was the place. Why would somebody go to this much trouble for a giant fence? It would have cost a lot to enclose a place like this. Why all the extra expense? Unless you were trying to hide something.

And he didn't know how, but there was one thing he was sure of.

Apollo was here.

30

DR. CATALYST CHASED APOLLO FOR TWO HOURS THAT night, until he finally cornered him near one of the old food stands. Apollo tried to bite him again, but he managed to grab the wiggling canine by the scruff of the neck. The little mutt had put up a valiant effort, but he was only a dog. Dr. Catalyst offered him a treat from his pocket, but Apollo refused to eat it, as if his judgment of Dr. Catalyst's character was final and not subject to appeal.

Dr. Catalyst was halfway back to the aquarium with Apollo in his arms when he realized something. The tablet. The dog didn't have it. Where had it gone? He hustled back inside the building and placed Apollo in the cage. He was taking no chance of letting him escape again.

Dr. Catalyst had a great deal of work to do before the morning. First, find the tablet. He went back outside and looked at the tracking screen: The red dot was stationary.

He walked to the spot where the GPS said it should be. It was an open area between the Poseidon's Log Flume ride and Sammy the Shrimp's House of Mirrors. He checked his phone again, and the dot started blinking. He cursed. He wasn't getting an accurate reading because the tablet was losing its charge. The mutt must have damaged it.

This was an inconvenience, but not a catastrophe. There was a second set of controls in the operations room at the aquarium. He could raise the cage manually and set the timer from the backup system.

He activated another application on his phone, which shut down the tablet remotely. Given its low power reading, he couldn't be sure it worked, but he would worry about that later. The chances of it being discovered were not great, and everything on it was encrypted and password protected.

Back in the aquarium, he struggled mightily to turn the crank on the winch that manually raised the cage. As he heaved and pulled, he cursed the entire Doyle family, including their dog. Finally, it was positioned over the tank. Apollo sat on his haunches, staring at Dr. Catalyst as he rose in the air. The mutt would not break eye contact, so Dr. Catalyst looked away. He removed the handle to the winch, taking it inside the control room, where he locked it in a cabinet. He then set the timer on the mechanism that would open the cage bottom.

The hour was growing late, and it was time to remove some of the Muraecudas out of the tank and deliver them to the ocean. Hopefully there was still enough darkness for cover. If there were more of them sighted before the deadline, if they attacked additional swimmers or caused more havoc, the governor and the task force would have to change their minds. Apollo would be saved.

Getting the creatures out of the tanks was relatively easy. The main tank had metal grates that lowered from the ceiling and sectioned it into three parts. When the aquarium was open and shows were going on, the trainers used these grates to herd the dolphins or seals into holding pens that were sectioned off from the main tanks by Plexiglas doors. These holding pens were out of sight beneath the bleachers and were where the animals were housed when there was no show. Each of the pens was accessible by tunnels beneath the aquarium so keepers and trainers could tend to the animals.

Dr. Catalyst had modified the holding pens, making them smaller so he could more easily remove the

Muraecudas. He pushed a button and one of the thick Plexiglas panels rose. At the rear of one of the pens he lowered a mesh bag filled with lionfish into the water. Water overflowed the sides of the pen as the hydrostatic pressure from the aquarium pushed it up and over. Drains in the floor collected the salt water, cleaned and filtered it, and pumped it back into the main tank.

Quicker than he could have ever imagined, six of the beasts swam into the pen, and he immediately lowered the gate. Their sense of smell was incredible. They were insatiable, ripping open the bag and devouring the fish.

Moving the Muraecudas was the most dangerous part of the job. They were vicious and ravenously hungry. Once one of them had slipped out of the net he used to transfer them from the pen. It landed on the floor, and even though it was out of the water, its body went berserk, jaws snapping as it tried to reach him. The Muraecudas were made to fight and feed, and he could not afford an accident. One lucky bite and he could bleed out before he could get help.

Finally, his work was complete and they were safely aboard the boat. Starting it up, he turned the bow south toward the ocean and disappeared into the darkness.

31

EMMET POUNDED ON THE GATE IN FRUSTRATION.

"He's here. I know it," he said. "Only there's no way in. I don't suppose you thought to bring a ladder, did you?"

"No," Calvin said. "But I did bring my cell phone. We could call my mom or Stuke's dad. Somebody could be here in minutes."

Emmet seriously considered it. He didn't care about getting in trouble. Apollo was all that mattered. But if they called and Apollo was not there, then they were in huge trouble regardless. Plus, they would have pulled them away from the search. He didn't know what to do.

"What's it going to be?" Calvin prodded him.

"Answer a question first. You're keeping something from me. What was Mrs. Clawson talking about? Something about Apollo and Dr. Catalyst. Please don't lie to me, Calvin. I need to know," Emmet said.

Calvin sighed. He punched a couple buttons on his phone and handed it to Emmet. It was a photo of Apollo suspended above the tank of Muraecudas.

"He posted another video. I overheard my mom talking about it. Don't get mad at her or your dad, Emmet. . . ."

"What? Why? What is he going to do?" Emmet was completely distraught.

"If the governor doesn't close the beaches and my mom doesn't close the Everglades and stop hunting the Pterogators by ten A.M., a timer will go off and the floor of the cage will open. Apollo —"

Emmet looked at the time on the phone. It was 9:45.

"Why didn't you tell me?"

"I thought they'd find him by now! Honest, I did! Everyone is looking! Off-duty policemen, firemen, volunteers . . . I thought —"

"There's no time to call now. How are we going to get in?"

Calvin shrugged out of his backpack and removed what looked like a giant pair of pliers from it.

"With these," he said. "The chain looks too thick, but it's all I've got." He slipped the blades over a link of the chain holding the gate shut. Of course the chain was high-quality tempered steel, but these would have to do.

"Who are you?" Emmet asked. "Why do you have bolt cutters?"

"They were my dad's," Calvin said as he groaned with the effort. "I have all of his tools. Right now I wish he'd owned a bigger pair of bolt cutters."

Emmet put his hands over Calvin's and pulled hard, wedging his feet against the gate and leaning back to gain as much leverage as possible. Using every bit of strength they possessed, they dug in. When the bolt cutters finally snapped through the chain, both of them tumbled to the ground.

"Hurry!" Emmet said, scrambling to his feet.

Pulling the chain from the gate, Emmet and Calvin opened it and charged through. Off to the south they saw the aquarium building, and they headed for it at a dead run. There was a ramped entrance on both ends of the rectangular building. The ramps led to the top of the amphitheater. From there, visitors had to enter the rows of bleachers. They headed left and raced up the concrete walkway, only to find their way blocked by a locked steel door. Emmet wanted to look at the time on his phone but was afraid to.

"Come on!" Emmet said, hurrying back down the ramp. Knowing the other ramp would lead to a similarly locked door, Emmet raced around toward the back of the building. There had to be other ways inside, like a staff entrance or emergency exits.

At the rear of the aquarium, right next to the construction fence, was another door. Just a regular, ordinary locked door. Calvin stepped forward, holding the bolt cutters in one hand, and swung with all his might. He hit the doorknob squarely and knocked it off completely. He jammed the head of the bolt cutters into the opening and, using them like a lever, put his weight into it and yanked on the handles. The door popped open.

Emmet pulled his phone from his pocket. It was now 9:50. They had ten minutes.

32

DR. CATALYST WAS SPEEDING BACK UP THE RIVER IN HIS boat. Last night's trip to release the Muraecudas had taken much longer than planned. Finding a suitable place had proven difficult. A storm was rising, and once he was out in the sound, the wind had picked up. The waves had gotten rough. The boat could handle them, but in order to safely free the creatures, the water needed to be relatively calm. If he opened the release panel on the bottom of the boat in high seas, the boat could take on too much water and founder before the pumps could clear the tank.

He had been forced to stay in the harbor longer than anticipated. All the while, he'd debated returning to the aquarium, but once he'd loaded the creatures onto the boat, he preferred to let them go. The harbor was not a suitable location, for the lionfish fed in deeper water, and if Dr. Catalyst's creatures nested there, it would be that much easier to capture and remove them.

The waters had finally calmed, and he'd piloted his boat into the sound, turning east toward Miami and the more popular beaches. The closer to the major metropolitan areas the better. Once the release was completed, he'd realized he had traveled a longer distance and would need to hustle to make it back to the aquarium.

Throughout the night he kept the onboard radio tuned to a local all-news station. He heard his name mentioned frequently in the discussions among the newscasters and journalists. But no word from the governor's office about closing the beaches or Everglades.

Part of him was not surprised. After all, he had put them in a difficult position. They did not understand his true intentions. Calling him a terrorist when he was in fact a brilliant scientist had only made matters much worse. It confused the issue. Instead of having a genuine discussion, or allowing the benefits of his work to take root, the system was out to stop him.

There was nothing he could do now. It wasn't as if he hadn't given them a chance. If they refused to listen, he was powerless. From here on out, anything that happened was on their shoulders.

As he traveled up the river, drawing near Undersea Land, Dr. Catalyst's phone buzzed in his pocket. The screen blinked, showing an alarm had been tripped at the aquarium. The phone was functioning as his tablet until he could secure a new one. He pulled up the on-site cameras and flipped through their feeds. In the control room he saw something truly shocking.

Emmet Doyle and Calvin Geaux. Calvin was sitting at the console, studying the board, and Emmet was gesturing wildly behind him.

He pulled back the throttle, and the boat sped up the river toward the dock. From a drawer in the console he removed a ski mask and placed it in a pocket of the blue coveralls he wore.

Somehow they had found him again.

33

AS SOON AS THEY RAN THROUGH THE DOOR, EMMET heard barking.

"Apollo!" Emmet shouted. Upon hearing Emmet, Apollo upped the barking to truly stupendous levels. Racing into the main arena, they saw the tank full of slithering Muraecudas and Apollo suspended in the cage above them.

"How are we going to get him down?" Emmet said.

"Don't know," said Calvin. He looked at the cage and the boom it hung from. An electric winch attached it to the aquarium wall. He sprinted over and studied the box, but the entire mechanism was enclosed inside the metal. He didn't see a switch or crank, or any way for it to be moved.

"There has to be a way to operate this thing in the control room," Calvin said. "Come on."

Emmet followed and stood behind him while he studied the controls. Calvin was good at mechanical stuff, but to Emmet, this console with its dozens of switches and blinking lights looked like something you'd find on a spaceship. He had no idea if Calvin could figure it out or not. Apollo's barking was making him crazy, so he sprinted back to the tank.

"Hey, buddy! How's my boy?" he shouted up to Apollo, who immediately stopped barking and wagged his tail.

"We're going to get you down! Don't worry!" he said. Apollo barked again, scratching at the cage with his paw. Emmet moved closer to the side of the tank.

Suddenly, one of the Muraecudas launched itself at him, hitting the glass with an alarmingly loud *thump*.

"Holy —!" Emmet jumped and scrambled backward. All he could see was a really ugly face and some of the largest, scariest teeth he'd ever encountered. They were longer than the Pterogators', and there were rows and rows of them. They jutted out of the creature's jaws at odd angles and protruded when it closed its mouth. The thing backed up and lunged forward, hitting the glass again. It shook its head as if stunned.

"Not so bright, are you?!" Emmet screamed at it.

The Muraecuda took no notice of his outrage, swimming away.

The time on Emmet's cell phone now said 9:59.

"Calvin! You better think of something!"

"I'm working on it!"

Emmet heard a whirring sound. He looked up to see the bottom of the cage flip open and Apollo tumble out, landing with a *splash* in the tank a few feet below.

Without thinking, Emmet scrambled up the side of the tank and dived into the water.

He was going to save his dog.

34

CALVIN WAS SO INTENT ON STUDYING THE BOARD before him, he didn't hear or see the man in the mask enter the control room. A bright red button labeled EMERGENCY PURGE had his full attention. He had no idea what it meant. Actually he had an idea, he just didn't know for sure if he should push the button.

The other reason he didn't hear the man come through the door was all the screaming Emmet was doing. The small monitor on the console showed the tank, and he had watched in horror as the bottom of the cage flipped open and Apollo tumbled into the water, followed immediately by Emmet scaling the side of the tank like a ninja and plunging in after him. Now Emmet was holding a sputtering Apollo in one arm, treading water with the other, and trying to keep his eyes on the Muraecudas that were circling ever closer.

Calvin felt something cold and metallic touch the back of his neck.

A voice said, "Slowly — very slowly — stand up and back away from the console."

Calvin knew who it was immediately. He would never forget that voice. He did as he was ordered and stood, his arms raised at the elbows. When he turned around there was a man in a ski mask, wearing blue coveralls and pointing a gun at him. Emmet had been right all along. It was definitely the same guy. He held the gun in his left hand this time, and the ring and pinkie fingers on his right were curled up and twisted. The Pterogator bite must have torn up the ligaments.

"What am I going to do with you two?" Dr. Catalyst said.

This was when Calvin wished Emmet were here. Emmet would say something snarky and get under Dr. Catalyst's skin. He would think of a diversion. That was not Calvin's game. He said the only thing he could think of.

"Let us go?"

"Hardly. But your friend in the tank has given me an idea. I think you should join him for a little swim. It will be interesting to see how long the two of you can last. . . ."

"You talk a lot," Calvin said. Dropping his arms, he kicked the chair between them at Dr. Catalyst, crashing it into him. Calvin spun around and pushed the Emergency Purge button. Loud alarms sounded. He could hear machinery humming to life and the pumps starting up, followed by the sounds of splashing water. He sprinted for the open door leading to the park. His first instinct had been to run toward Emmet. But if they split up, Dr. Catalyst wouldn't be able to control them both as easily. Besides, he wasn't going far.

"No!" Dr. Catalyst shouted. He pounded on the console, flipping switches and punching buttons.

Once Calvin cleared the door, he darted to the side of it and pulled the bolt cutters from his backpack. A few seconds later, he heard Dr. Catalyst coming after him, abandoning his efforts with the controls. It was just as Calvin hoped. When the arm holding the gun appeared through the doorway, Calvin swung the bolt cutters down like a club, connecting on Dr. Catalyst's arm with a resounding *crack*.

Dr. Catalyst screamed and dropped the gun. Calvin picked it up and stuffed it in his backpack while Dr. Catalyst fell to his knees, groaning in pain. Calvin scurried back inside, through the control room, toward the main tank. As he ran, he pulled his phone from his pocket and pushed the emergency button. His mom had the phone preprogrammed with numbers for all the agencies involved in the hunt for Dr. Catalyst. An operator answered on the first ring.

"My name is Calvin Geaux. My mother is Dr. Rosalita Geaux, superintendent of the Everglades National Park. I'm at the old Undersea Land amusement park, south of Florida City. We need people here ASAP! Dr. Catalyst is here and he's armed and there's a fire and I think there might be a chemical weapon. I have to hang up now to help my friend." Calvin didn't want to leave anything to chance. His mom had said the county 9-1-1 operators were supposed to dispatch police to any Dr. Catalyst threat without hesitation.

Inside he found the tank almost empty. Emmet was standing on the bottom, knee-deep in water. A ton of sea water had spilled over the sides and was now running into drains all around the concrete. Calvin could only guess, but apparently the Emergency Purge emptied the tank in case a trainer fell in or an animal was injured and they needed to get to it in a hurry.

Emmet was still kicking and screaming at the Muraecudas that swam too close in the shallow water, but the remaining water drained rapidly. A few seconds later, it was too shallow for them to swim at all, and they flopped about on the floor of the tank.

"Don't move!" Calvin shouted. "Those things can still bite! And hold on to Apollo!"

"What did you do?" Emmet shouted up to him. The noise of the pumps was deafening. They had to be extremely powerful to remove so many gallons of water so quickly.

"I don't know! I pushed the Emergency Purge button!"

"Did you know that's what it did?"

"No!"

"Good plan!"

"I thought you'd like it!"

35

"**I** DON'T REMEMBER, EXACTLY," EMMET WAS SAYING to Dr. Geaux and his dad, as he sat in the back of an ambulance.

"I went over the side. The water was way cold. Apollo popped to the surface, and I swam to him. Those creatures were confused at first. Probably all they've been fed is lionfish, and we don't resemble them. It was like they didn't know what he was, and I got to him before they could figure out we were food. I held on to Apollo with one arm and treaded water with the other. Those things attacked and attacked. I remembered that day in the ocean and just kept kicking them in the face whenever they got close. It was all I could think to do. I knew Calvin would figure out a way to save us."

Dr. Geaux was pacing back and forth. Emmet wasn't sure, but he thought from the look on her face that he and Calvin were going to be in big trouble. His dad just looked relieved.

She looked at Calvin. Then at Emmet.

"You two!" she said. "What part of 'Don't get involved in this' do you not understand?"

Apollo was in Emmet's lap, wrapped in a towel. He looked up at her and barked.

"Don't you start," she said to Apollo.

"Dr. Geaux, I'm sorry. And I understand why you're mad. But Dr. Catalyst took my dad *and* my dog. And that kind of involves me. And if Calvin hadn't come with me, I'd be dead. I say we call it a win and go home," Emmet said. He was trying very hard to sound cheerful and nonchalant about the whole ordeal. Part of him felt bad for making them worry. But he couldn't sit by, either.

"Do you know what could have happened to you?" She had switched to angry-mom mode. Emmet and Calvin said nothing. They just looked down at the ground. Finally, Emmet looked back up at her.

"I could have gotten eaten. Or chewed up pretty good. But we stopped him again," Emmet pointed out.

"Don't think that gets you off the hook," Dr. Doyle said. "Rosalita is right, you could've —"

"And if you'd called us, we might have been able to

apprehend him. Instead he got away again, and who knows what he's going to do next!" Dr. Geaux said.

Apollo barked and jumped out of Emmet's lap. He ran off, disappearing around the Princess of Atlantis ride.

"Where's he going now?" Emmet asked.

The four of them trotted after him, and were met by Apollo coming back toward them, a ten-inch tablet computer in his mouth.

He laid it at Dr. Geaux's feet.

"What do you suppose this is?" Dr. Geaux said, picking it up carefully by the edges with just her forefingers.

"I don't know," Emmet said. "But I've got a pretty good idea who it belongs to."

Epilogue

STUKE'S DAD LED THE POLICE INTO DR. NEWTON'S HOUSE.
When he heard Emmet's story, his police car practically flew to the address. Emmet and Calvin followed in Dr. Geaux's car, with Dr. Doyle riding shotgun. Apollo refused to leave Emmet's lap.

They waited out on the street while Lieutenant Stukaczowski and three other officers went up to the front door, guns drawn, ready to confront Dr. Newton. Everyone finally believed he was Dr. Catalyst. Emmet admitted to having seen an identical tablet in Dr. Newton's briefcase, which was the clincher for Dr. Geaux. She even overlooked the fact that Emmet had been poking around in Dr. Newton's private stuff.

Police cars were scattered all around the street, their

lights flashing. The four of them waited for Stuke's dad to reappear with Dr. Newton in handcuffs.

Calvin had been unusually quiet during the ride, like he was thinking very hard about something. Emmet had come to recognize the look.

"What's on your mind?" Emmet asked quietly. Dr. Geaux and his dad were talking on cell phones to other task-force members.

"Dr. Catalyst. He . . . his right arm was injured. I noticed it right away. His ring and pinkie finger were curled up, like the ligaments had been damaged. And he held the gun in his left hand this time," Calvin said.

"So?" Emmet said.

"So he wasn't wearing a cast on his arm. It was obviously injured, but no cast. Not like Dr. Newton."

Emmet thought about this for a minute.

"Maybe the cast was removable. To throw people off. Like in the movies. It makes a good disguise," Emmet said.

"Maybe," Calvin said. He went back to thinking.

The policemen didn't come back for several minutes. When they did reappear, none of them was leading Dr. Newton along in handcuffs. Much to Emmet's chagrin.

"Where is he?" Emmet asked.

"He's not here," Lieutenant Stukaczowski said. "Dr. Geaux, I called the FBI and had my men pull out of the apartment."

"The FBI? Do you think he's on the run?" Dr. Geaux asked.

He shook his head. "I don't think so. I don't think he left by choice."

"What do you mean?" Emmet said.

"There are signs of a struggle inside. Chairs tipped over, books and magazines pushed off tables and onto the floor. And worse, there's blood on the kitchen counter . . . like someone hit their head or was injured in a fight," he said.

He removed his uniform hat and ran his hands over his short red hair.

"If I had to guess, I'd say Dr. Newton has been kidnapped."

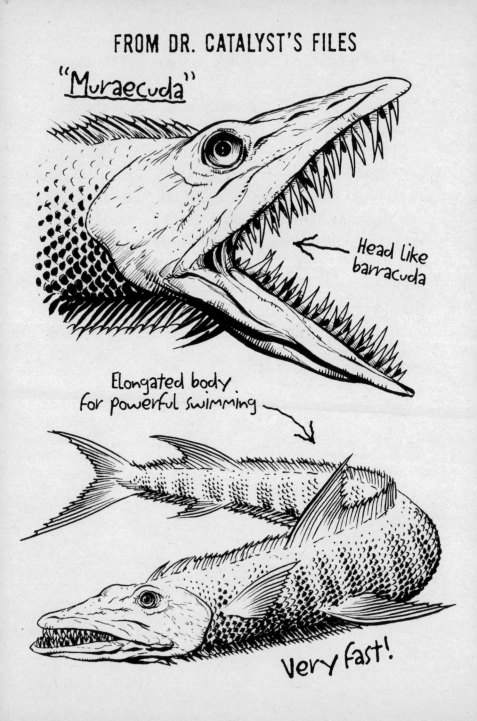

Rows of piercing teeth

MUST BE CAREFUL

NEVER AGAIN

Size and muscle of reef shark

A sneak peek of the next
KILLER SPECIES

out for blood

Late September

IT HAD COME TO THIS.

Dr. Catalyst piloted the boat silently through the Aerojet Canal outside of Florida City. It was nearing midnight, and the sky was full of rain clouds. He was moving through the water on low power with no lights. Though it was unlikely his enemies would ever manage to capture him, he was still a wanted fugitive and took every precaution.

His advance planning and well-reasoned strategies had led him to this moment. A few weeks ago, his latest efforts at combating the invasive species infesting South Florida had been thwarted again by Emmet Doyle and Calvin Geaux. Dr. Catalyst glanced down at his mangled right hand, something else he had Emmet and Calvin to thank for. In the Everglades, Emmet had induced a Pterogator to attack him, and its bite had nearly severed his arm. Now he had lost access to his Pterogators and Muraecudas. And not only that, Emmet's stupid dog had bitten him. Repeatedly. He was tired, aching, and angry.

Dr. Catalyst was through with subtlety. He was finished with taking a measured approach. Those in power did not see the value of his methods. Man had introduced vile, destructive creatures into the fragile ecosystem and the only way to heal it was to create a new level of predators to eliminate them. All he was asking was to be left alone to save the environment.

The boat slowed to a stop, floating gently in the middle of the canal. A few weeks ago, he had come to this very spot to kidnap Emmet Doyle's dog, Apollo. The Doyle home backed up to the canal and was close to the Everglades. Remembering that night made his damaged hand and dog-bitten calf muscle ache, reminding him of his failure.

On the boat's rear deck was a large Plexiglas construct, roughly the size of a phone booth. Small holes were drilled in the sides to allow in oxygen for the creatures inside. Dr. Catalyst put on a helmet with a clear plastic face shield. He was wearing thick gloves and canvas overalls. As he approached the container, the animals within it flapped leathery wings and a chittering rose from inside.

He placed his gloved hands on the clear plastic, and the captured creatures swarmed at them, thumping against the side. Loud screeching sounds replaced the chittering. Dr. Catalyst could make out one of the creatures in the din, flapping wings with long, sharp claws at their end. Its face was a horror of small sharp teeth and huge dark eyes, plus a pair of insectlike antennae. The creature's wings tucked in as it stretched toward him, revealing not four spindly limbs, but six. There were hundreds just like it in the container, small in size, but very belligerent. And they were hungry.

Unbelievably hungry.

Once again he had combined two species into one. Each was aggressive in its own right. The vampire bat was a nocturnal hunter that required drinking over 60 percent of its body weight in mammalian blood each night in order to survive. The baldfaced hornet was among the most aggressive members of the yellow-jacket family. They could bite as well as sting, and would protect their nests with utmost ferocity. With his revolutionary gene splicing, growth hormones, and his technique for recombining DNA from divergent species, Dr. Catalyst had created the ideal invasive species.

Yes.

An invasive species.

He was releasing his own nonnative animals into South Florida. His Pterogators and Muraecudas had served a specific purpose: to rid the Everglades and the ocean of snakes and lionfish.

But his newest creations were here for only one reason: to create havoc.

If no one would willingly accept his methods, he would show them the negative impact of an invasive species firsthand. And before long his latest creations would find sustenance from the most prevalent warm-blooded mammals in Florida.

Humans.

Dr. Catalyst stepped inside the cabin of the boat. He had rigged a cable release, attached to a pulley system, which allowed the creatures to be set free from inside where it was safe. Still, he wore the helmet and thick coveralls as a precaution.

Taking a breath, he pushed a lever forward, and through a hole drilled in the cabin wall, the cable pulled open the top of the cage. For a moment, nothing happened. Then, with a rush of wings and loud piercing squeals, they exploded into the night sky. Dozens of the creatures threw themselves at the cabin window, then more followed, trying to reach him through the glass. Their savageness caused Dr. Catalyst to draw back from the sight of them. Unable to breach the cabin, they finally gave up and flew upward, joining hundreds of their brethren in the sky.

From here they would spread out and begin nesting. Colonies would form and they would terrorize the population of Florida City.

They would own the night.

A few of the things about dogs is they eat a lot, sleep a lot, and if they were Apollo — with a sense of smell and hearing he considered superior to every living creature, including other dogs — they were obsessive about needing to go outside a lot. Ever since he was taken captive by Dr. Catalyst, Apollo woke up several times a night, wanting to investigate the backyard. It was as if he had a score to settle with his onetime captor.

It was almost midnight, according to the clock on Emmet's bedroom desk. Apollo was standing on Emmet's chest, licking his face and making a soft growling sound. Emmet tried rolling over and burying himself with pillows and blankets. No use. Apollo dug through and found Emmet's face again, where he went to work licking and yipping quietly. Either he had to go, or he'd heard something outside that needed investigation. And Emmet would get no rest until Apollo was sure the backyard was secure.

Sitting up, Emmet rubbed the sleep from his eyes. Apollo sat back on his haunches, pleased that Emmet now understood what was required of him. He ran his hand over Apollo's ears and scratched gently. Next to food of nearly any kind, this was the dog's most favorite thing. Emmet felt Apollo's collar, making sure it was securely attached, and checking the special "dog license" medallion secured to it.

After Dr. Catalyst kidnapped Apollo, Dr. Geaux had gone to the FBI and obtained a unique fob for Apollo's license. It looked like a regular dog license, but it contained a special chip in it that would allow them to track Apollo, were he to be captured again.

"I don't suppose I could talk you out of this, could I?" Emmet asked. Apollo cocked his head and gave a quiet yip.

"Couldn't you at least bark loud enough to wake up Dad? Then he could take you outside," Emmet grumbled. "Come on."

He stood up, stretched, and stumbled groggily for his bedroom door. Outside he heard thunder rumble off in the distance. The wind was making a weird sound on the roof of the house. A storm must be coming. Apollo ran ahead of him to the backdoor and scratched at it eagerly.

"Hold your horses," Emmet groused. "You shouldn't

drink so much water before you go to bed. I've got school tomorrow, you know."

There was a brand-new alarm system pad next to the door. Emmet entered the code, and it beeped as it was deactivated. When he opened the door, Apollo catapulted through it and rushed across the small patio to the grass, nose down, working the ground like a bloodhound. Emmet often wondered what it must be like to have the millions of scents in the world pulling you in a different direction every few seconds.

Ever since Dr. Catalyst had snatched Apollo, Emmet stood in the doorway and watched over him while he was outside. He still had nightmares and horrible flashbacks of Apollo tumbling into the tank full of Muraecudas. He was determined that madman would never get his hands on Apollo again, so the little black mutt got a wingman whenever he had to visit the backyard.

Apollo sniffed his way along the ground to the first of the three cypress trees that grew in the yard. Emmet watched him through hooded eyes, still groggy with sleep. The wind picked up, and off to the west the sky lit up with lightning. Over the breeze, he heard a whispering sound above his head on the roof of the house. For a moment he thought it sounded like bird wings. *I need sleep*, Emmet thought. *Hurry up, Apollo*.

Now the dog was sniffing hard at the trunk of the tree. He went up on his hind legs, his forepaws planted against the trunk of the tree. Emmet groaned. He hoped it wasn't a raccoon. He could be out here all night. He flipped on the outdoor lights.

"Apollo, come," he said. Apollo ignored the command.

And barked. Loudly.

"Apollo," Emmet hissed. "Come on, let's go!"

Apollo was unmoved.

Emmet left the doorway, the screen door slamming behind him, and trotted to the tree. Apollo darted away.

"Oh, come on!" Emmet complained. The strange whispering noise was louder now. From the corner of his eye, he thought he saw something dark fly low across the ground, from the tree toward the roof of the house. It must have been a bird. Nothing drove Apollo nuts like birds.

While he was chasing Apollo, another bird flew from the tree to the roof and Apollo pursued it. When Emmet turned around to follow his dog, he suddenly saw that the roof of their house was covered with birds. They were flapping their wings and hopping about, making a strange chittering sound. Florida had hundreds of bird species. Nighttime was a symphony of animal noises, from birds to frogs to alligators bellowing in the canal behind their house. But he had yet to hear the call of this one. To Emmet it almost sounded like bees in a hive. Maybe it was some kind of seasonal migration no one had bothered to warn him about.

As he trailed Apollo toward the house, the sound changed from a low-pitched hum to a high screech. Emmet skidded to a stop in the yard. Apollo was in a barking frenzy. Now that he was close enough to see the roof clearly in the light, Emmet froze in fear.

These were not birds roosting on the rooftop of their house.

They were bats.

A whole lot of bats. Hundreds of them. And as Emmet shouted in alarm, they rose as one into the night sky, wings flapping. A horrible shriek rose over the noise of the wind. Terrified, Emmet wanted to run but was rooted in place.

"Dad! Dad! Hurry!" he shouted as loud as he could.

The bats circled briefly in the air above him. Then, like something out of the most frightening horror movie he had ever seen, they turned in flight.

And they dived directly toward him.

Out of the darkness, heroes will rise...

Also Available:

by
Kathryn
Huang

by
Kathryn
Huang &
Kathryn
Lasky

Read them all!

SCHOLASTIC

www.scholastic.com/gahoole

GAHOOLE15

THERE'S NOWHERE TO HIDE.

INFESTATION

SOMETHING HUGE IS ON THE MARCH

TIMOTHY J. BRADLEY

SCHOLASTIC

Andy knew that reform school would mean cruel drill
instructors and brutal bullies, but he wasn't prepared
for an endless swarm of giant mutant ants!

scholastic.com

Available in print
and eBook editions

INFEST